Love LETTERS

An award-winning author, Anne Cassidy has written over twenty books for teenagers. She is fascinated by the way ordinary people can be sucked into crime and forced to make agonizing moral decisions.

Praise for Anne Cassidy's books:

"Totally gripping" *Books for Keeps*
"Dark, chilling and clever . . . Anne Cassidy reminds me of Minette Walters or Ruth Rendell" CELIA REES
"Always compelling" *Telegraph*
"Compassionate and unflinching" *Guardian*, JAN MARK

anne cassidy

Love LETTERS

SCHOLASTIC

First published in 2003 by Scholastic Children's Books
An imprint of Scholastic Ltd
Euston House, 24 Eversholt Street
London, NW1 1DB, UK
Registered office: Westfield Road, Southam, Warwickshire, CV47 0RA
SCHOLASTIC and associated logos are trademarks and or registered trademarks of
Scholastic Inc.

Cover photograph © Corbis

10 digit ISBN 0 439 95096 1
13 digit ISBN 978 0439 95096 1

British Library Cataloguing-in-Publication Data.
A CIP catalogue record for this book is available from the British Library

Printed in the UK by CPI Bookmarque, Croydon, CR0 4TD
Papers used by Scholastic Children's Books are made from wood grown in
sustainable forests.

5 7 9 10 8 6 4

www.scholastic.co.uk/zone

ONE

The first letter came on a Friday morning, the last day at college that half term. It was in a bright blue envelope that felt thick and expensive and I held it in my hand for a few moments before opening it. I wasn't used to getting *personal* letters. I got bank statements, junk mail from a computer company, leaflets from a book club I'd once been a member of and the odd letter of information from college. Nothing else. Certainly not a love letter.

I'd just finished eating my breakfast and I was standing at the kitchen table, tidying up my college bag, placing my folders in the order in which I had my lessons and putting my highlighter pens back in their case. My mum marched in carrying the post. She was wearing one of her suits, a dark brown matching skirt and jacket with a crisp white blouse underneath. She quickly thumbed through the letters, casting aside the junk mail. She handed the blue envelope to me and then started to clear the breakfast things off the table.

The notepaper was a matching blue, carefully folded to fit the envelope exactly. The letter had been typed and was in an unusual font, the kind that looks like neat handwriting.

Dear Victoria,

I love you.

X X X

Only the kisses had been handwritten.

It pleased me, I can't deny it. I read it over several times and it made me smile in a silly girlie way, quite unlike me really. At that point I had no idea who had sent it, but that didn't make it any less special. Someone admired me, liked me, had a secret longing for me. I turned the envelope over and there, in the same font, was my full name, *Victoria Halladay*, and my address, every bit, right down to the postcode. I found myself sitting up straight, thrusting my chest out and combing my fingers through my hair.

"Anything interesting?" my mum said, leaning against the work surface, her fingers flicking through the pages of her diary.

"Just something," I said, mysteriously.

My dad came in then. He was wearing his usual suit and tie, his shoes polished, his heels clicking on the kitchen tiles. Underneath his arm were a couple of envelope folders.

"You ready?" he said to me.

I nodded, fitting my box of disks and my mobile phone into the zip-up pocket on the front of my bag. Then I picked up the letter and, without folding it, put it carefully into my jeans back pocket.

My dad jangled his keys and looked over at my mum.

"What time do you finish today, Barb?"

"About five. Five thirty?" she said.

"I won't be in until about seven."

"OK," my mum said, closing her diary.

He gave her a kiss and I gave a little wave. Then I followed him out of the door and towards his car, thinking all the time about the mysterious letter. In my head the names of several boys I knew lined up. I focused on each one for a second, trying to imagine the matching blue paper and envelope, the neat print, the brief but stunning phrase, *I love you*. It wasn't the sort of thing that I could imagine anybody I knew writing. There was someone I would have *liked* it to be but I pushed his name to the back of my mind and let the other names jostle for position. I knew that Jen and I would replay them all later.

In the car, the music was very loud.

"Dad!" I said, putting my hands over my ears.

"I love this one!" he said, jiggling about in the seat, using his fingers like drumsticks on the steering wheel. For a head teacher and a parent my dad could be a total embarrassment sometimes.

"This is an important time for Mum," my dad said loudly, turning into the road where the college was.

"I know." I raised my voice.

He pulled the car over to the kerb and I got my stuff together. Just as I was about to open the door he lowered the volume and started to speak.

"This job means a lot to her. It'll be good for all of us.

There'll be extra money. We'll need that, especially when you go to uni."

"I know."

I was impatient to get out and go and find Jen. Closing the car door I stood and waved as my dad drove off. Then I headed for the main doors of the college. I patted my back pocket, feeling the satisfying crinkle of my first ever love letter. It needed to be opened up, read again, talked about, interpreted. Fortunately my best friend was in her usual seat in the canteen. In front of her were an apple and a satsuma and a cup of black coffee.

"Beginnings of a diet," she said, before I asked. "Just want to get a few pounds off before Christmas. Got to get into that party dress."

She patted her stomach and gazed at the two pieces of fruit sitting sparsely in front of her.

I made myself comfortable on the seat opposite. Jen was always going on diets and usually coming off them just as quick. She wasn't fat, far from it. She was rounder than me, though, her breasts and hips bigger, her arms and legs solid. Her face was full and her cheeks dimpled when she smiled. I thought she was really attractive. She thought she was fat. That's why she carried, in the front of her bag, a *Handy Calorie Counter*, which meant that each of us knew the calorific value of most foods up to the nearest ten.

"That your breakfast?"

"Breakfast, my foot. That's my lunch," she said mournfully.

I pulled the blue envelope out of my back pocket and handed it to her. I watched as she opened it, read it and turned the paper over and back, finally reading the words out loud.

"*Dear Victoria, I love you*. What's this?"

"Some secret admirer."

I got a breakfast bar out of my bag and began to unpeel the wrapping. The bar was brown and mottled and looked like baked sawdust. In fact it tasted sweet and was rather nice. Jen looked at it and then back at the letter.

"Three hundred and twenty calories. Who sent it?"

"I don't know! That's the point!" I said, mildly exasperated.

"Oh!" she said, the penny dropping.

I left her making a list of possibles while I got myself a cup of tea from the counter. Across the canteen I saw Ricky Fairfax, a boy from my tutor group who was always chatting to me and Jen. He waved at me and I nodded back at him, paid for my tea and walked back towards Jen. When I sat down again I saw that she had a number of names written on a corner of her pad. I looked at them as if from a great distance. I didn't think any of them capable of such a gesture. I blew the steam from the top of my tea and took a sip. It was hotter than molten lava so I put it down to let it cool.

"What about Carl Ritter?" Jen said, holding her pad up as though it was a clipboard.

"Nope, he can't write," I said.

"Don't be unkind! He was nice."

Poor Carl. He had hung around for a few months at the end of school. I'd gone out with him once but he'd been so keen. It had put me off.

"Dave Tooley?"

"No!" I said, in an astonished voice.

Dave Tooley was a boy from my street. I had had a crush on him for weeks. We'd got together at a party and he'd kissed me a few times. I'd quite enjoyed it but when it stopped it was obvious that we had nothing to say to each other.

"Jordan Hill. What about him?"

That was going back a few years. In year seven or eight, I think, Jordan Hill had had a thing for me. He'd walked me home from school for a few weeks and bought me a Christmas present. I wasn't really girlfriend material, though, and it had embarrassed me, so I'd ended up trying to avoid him. He'd got quite upset, as I remembered, and my mum had gone round to talk to his mum. Then he'd got into the school football team and stopped bothering.

"I shouldn't think so."

That was the list. I wasn't exactly inundated with admirers. Jen picked up the satsuma and started to peel it. She saw me watching.

"Sixty calories. I can get another piece of fruit for lunch." She looked like she was thinking hard, "It's funny that he's used your full name. *Victoria*. Hardly anyone calls you that."

I perked up. Her words sunk in. *Dear Victoria*. Not Vicky or Vick, but my full name, *Victoria*.

"What about Ricky Fairfax? He calls you Victoria. And he likes you! He's always hanging round."

"No!" I said loudly enough for kids on the other table to hear.

"I'll bet it is. And I don't know why you're turning your nose up. He's nice," Jen said, taking her time, pulling the white pith from each segment of the satsuma.

I watched her eating for a moment and then looked around the cafeteria, averting my eyes from the part of the room where Ricky Fairfax was sitting with some friends. Ever since the letter arrived I'd not let myself think about the one important person who called me Victoria, even though he knew everyone else used the short version.

Chris Stoker. Jen's brother. I'd known him for years but in the last few weeks, since he and his long-term girlfriend had finished, I'd started to feel odd in his presence: self-conscious; delighted when he was there, strangely empty when he was out. He was older, and often seemed to be busy, but he always made a particular point of talking to me.

"Can I get you a cup of tea, Victoria?"

"So, what's happening, Victoria?"

"Whose heart you breaking these days, Victoria?"

He made me drinks, or offered beans on toast which seemed to be the only thing he could cook. I hardly dared think that it might be him. But why not? This wasn't the kind of thing done by a kid. It needed to be someone mature, confident with themselves. Most likely the letter wasn't meant to be read literally. It was like putting "Love" on a birthday card. It meant you had high regard for someone. Why not?

I felt pleased with myself, as though I had cracked a great mystery. It had to be from Chris Stoker. Who else was there? Just then Ricky Fairfax got up from his table and walked out of the canteen. I looked away quickly before he waved at me again.

"Perhaps he'll sign the next one," Jen said.

The next one. I thought about it for a moment. I hadn't considered that. A picture jumped into my head of Chris Stoker, sitting at a computer, a piece of blue notepaper threaded into the printer. The idea gave me a thrill.

If I had known then that there would be another letter, and others after that, I might not have felt so good. I picked up the blue paper, folded it and placed it back in the envelope. I might not have been so pleased with myself.

TWO

I didn't get the second letter until two weeks later. I was in my tutor room, sitting with a couple of girls who were in the same history group as me. They were talking about Hitler and the Nazis and I was half listening and half wondering why Jen was so late. I kept looking out of the window to see if she was coming. From our room I could see the college gates and the nearby bus stop but there was no sign of her. My tutor, Bob, was having trouble with the electronic register, bouncing his fingers off the buttons and heaving sigh after sigh, when the classroom door opened and one of the women from reception came in.

"Is Victoria Halladay here?" she said, completely ignoring Bob and looking around.

I stood up, a prickle of worry at the back of my neck. In school, the appearance of one of the admin staff always signalled trouble. Someone had to see the head, or there was some bad news from home. The woman from reception nodded her head at me and walked smartly across the classroom, her tight skirt making her footsteps short and quick. She smiled as she handed me the bright blue letter and I took it with a feeling of relief. It was not bad news, and I felt silly because I'd thought it might have been. I glanced down at the envelope. This time it was not my home address, but my name followed by the sign for "care of" and then the address of the college.

Sitting down, I made my face as blank as I could, trying to hide the mixture of surprise and pleasure I was feeling. I caught Ricky Fairfax's eye and I looked away, trying to act as normal as possible.

The first letter had made a big impact on me, I can't deny it. It had sent me into numerous soppy daydreams, imagining myself and Chris Stoker in some passionate relationship: holding hands, kissing, lying together on a sofa. But as every day went by and nothing else happened I began to feel a bit foolish about it. I know what I hoped – that Chris would give me a sign of some sort that he had been the sender. But nothing like that happened, and when the feeling of foolishness began to fade I got cross. I went to college, I did my work, I went to my job as a checkout assistant and I spent time with Jen. All the time there was this feeling of annoyance niggling away at me. It hadn't been Chris Stoker after all. It had been a joke. The sender was watching me from afar and was laughing at me. Something that had made me feel nice had turned into something that made me feel stupid. In the end I tried to forget about it. I tucked it away in a file in my head that said *April Fool*, even though it was early November.

But now there was a second letter. The two girls I'd been sitting with had stopped talking about the Third

Reich and were looking at the envelope pointedly. I held it for a moment, not wanting to open it there in front of them. Just then Bob Murphy slammed the lid of the electronic register down, making everyone look round.

"I can't get a connection. You lot go to your classes and I'll do this later."

I put the unopened letter in my bag, took a last look through the window to see if Jen was running up the college driveway and then went off to my first lesson.

Where the opposite sex were concerned I was not what you'd call *experienced*. Neither Jen or I had been one of the grown-up crowd at school, the girls who had breasts and hips from an early age, who wore the latest clothes and had more make-up than pens in their school bags. We were late starters, with more interest in our lives at school than our sex lives. We were boffin types, listening to and enjoying lessons, writing the homework neatly in our diaries and rushing off to the library at lunch time to do it. We both loved getting our books back from teachers with neat lines of red writing praising our efforts, and if there was a grade, with a little plus sign beside it, then even better.

When other girls were applying eyeliner and lipgloss we were using felt tips to colour in maps and draw posters. When they were reading problem-page letters out we were writing our novel about two orphan girls who joined the circus and became trapeze artists. When the girls crowded round to look at a Valentine card, or hear the details of some snogging session, Jen and I were filling in our French crosswords or struggling through a scene from a Shakespeare play.

We were disdainful of those girls. For us boys were big, loud, smelly things with grubby faces and dirty laughs. The ones who weren't like that were small and weedy; their voices squeaked and their bags were full of computer games.

We were above it all, and generally people left us alone.

Then one Monday, halfway through year eleven, Jen came into school with a bright red mark on her neck.

"It's a love bite," she whispered.

I was shocked. Not because I *disapproved*, but because I hadn't expected such a development. In my hand I had a rough draft of a chapter of a new novel we were supposed to be working on, where our heroine had magic powers. My interest in it vanished in the face of Jen's love bite.

"My cousin, Sam? You remember? He came with his mum at the weekend and stayed over. My brother Chris was there with his girlfriend, Karen, and we had some cans of lager and played cards. Sam and me, we. . ."

She stopped and I shoved the chapter back into my bag, the pages slipping awkwardly and folding over at the corners. I didn't care. I moved closer to Jen, sucked in by her story.

"He put his tongue in my mouth and his hand here. . ."

She pointed to one of her breasts and I felt a quivering feeling in my stomach.

"Then he gave me this!" she said, pointing to the raw mark on her neck.

"What did Chris say?" I said, shocked.

Her brother Chris was two years older. In fact he was her half-brother, and lived with his mum for most of the time, but he often stayed over at Jen's and she was always complaining that he bossed her about.

"He was snogging Karen. I could see him. He was licking her neck. Yuck."

I'd been dumbstruck.

"But you're cousins!"

It was all I could bring myself to say. In my chest, though, there was this ballooning envy. Jen and I simply weren't interested in boys that way. We hardly ever mentioned sex or any of those things. We were interested in more important matters like writing books and getting good grades and being Best at Things.

Then, overnight, she had gone off in a different direction, and instead of being mad at her I found myself resentful of what she'd done, jealous of the things she had experienced. I made her describe it to me all day long, over and over, every moment, every detail. It was as if I had been one of them, playing cards, drinking lager, and yet inside I had this big empty space because I hadn't been there. I was hungry. Then, after a final long phone call with Jen I'd gone to bed and found myself unable to sleep. I was twisted up in the sheets, the duvet up to my neck and then flung aside, the pillows high and then low. My legs were restless, folding up and straightening out;

even my skin felt strange, as if it had woken up from a long sleep, tingling, making me want to touch it.

We didn't change completely. We still looked about the same, Jen, tall and solid, her breasts big and full, her hair a reddish brown; me, smallish and thin, my hair yellowy, my skin pale, my smile hindered by a gap between my two front teeth. There were subtle differences, though. My uniform was washed and ironed more carefully. My underwear became more slight, more silky. My out-of-school clothes had the right labels.

We still worked hard and got good grades, but there was a restlessness about us, our eyes darting round, looking to see who had come into a room, who was with who, what was going on.

Jen still had a thing with her cousin Sam. He lived in Norfolk, though, so it was a relationship that depended on odd weekends and visits and a lot of phone calls and text-messaging. Me, I had a couple of brushes with the opposite sex, but none of it filled the hunger I felt on that day when Jen had told me about the game of cards and showed me her love bite. When Jen was going on and on about her sessions with Sam, or trying to find someone for me to fix my sights on, I was vague and restless. Except for her brother, Chris, there was no one I really liked.

When I got to my lesson I made a point of sitting at the back of the room on my own. I took the blue envelope out of my bag and opened it carefully, my hands as steady as a rock, my breath trembling in the back of my throat.

Dear Victoria,

   I love the way you look, your blonde hair and grey eyes. I even like the space between your teeth. You're innocent. That's why I love you.

                    X X X

My face broke into a smile. How silly of me to get so much pleasure out of a few words on a page.

THREE

Just before the end of the lesson Jen came rushing in mumbling apologies to the teacher. She looked around for me, then hurried up to the back of the room and squeezed into a space that was far too small for her to sit in comfortably. All the while she was making faces at me with her finger over her lips. I couldn't make head nor tail of it, and anyway I was still stuck in a kind of reverie, thinking about the second love letter.

In the corridor she blurted it all out.

"Talk about drama," she said. "We've had such a night of it! That's why I'm late."

"What's happened?" I asked, only mildly interested. Jen's family were always experiencing dramatic events.

"In the middle of the night there's this banging on the door. You know, like a there's a fire somewhere and we've all got to get up and get out. My dad goes down and it's Chris, standing there, with his bag, in a state."

"Chris?" I said, perking up.

"His stepdad's chucked him out. He's coming to live with us!"

I opened my mouth to speak, but when nothing came out I closed it again. Jen took hold of the sleeve of my jacket and pulled me in the direction of the cafeteria.

"I need a drink," she said. "I'm parched. I've had no

breakfast. Not with all the comings and goings. Come on, I'll tell you about it."

After a long queue and a few snippets of information we sat down. I had a cup of hot chocolate, 150 calories, and Jen had a black coffee, nil calories, and a bread roll with low-fat spread, 90 calories. While eating and drinking she told me the whole story over again. I listened avidly. Some of the stuff she said I already knew but I didn't stop her. I was fascinated by Chris's history and I didn't mind hearing it over.

When Jen's dad broke up with his first wife she had custody of Chris. Both of them remarried. Jen's dad had had Jen but Chris's mum hadn't had any other children, she'd just brought Chris up and concentrated on her career. The family lived a few miles from Jen's and Chris visited his dad a lot, staying over for weekends or spending holidays with them. Chris seemed OK with his mum and stepdad until he got older and the arguments started.

Jen loved Chris, admired him, looked up to him. There was only two years' difference but she thought of him as her own personal grown-up.

He was in the middle of a gap year, doing a couple of part-time jobs to give himself some money. Then he was going to do architecture at university.

But things at home had got worse. A couple of months before Chris had broken up with his long-term girlfriend and had been quite low. He'd lost one of his jobs and hung around the house a lot. Jen said he'd become a bit of slob and didn't seem to care about anything. His stepdad hadn't liked this, and relations between them deteriorated. Chris began to spend more time round his dad's, and it was during this time that I got to know him a bit better.

The night before, Jen said, with some relish, there'd been a terrible argument. Chris's stepdad had caught him smoking in his room and hit the roof. There was a big argument with a lot of pointing and shouting. Chris swore at his stepdad, telling him to get out of his room. His stepdad then told Chris to get out of the house. Chris's mum tried to calm everything but it didn't work and Chris walked out. Jen stopped at this point and looked at me with absolute incredulity. *He walked out, in the middle of the night!* she repeated, shaking her head.

It didn't end there. When Chris arrived at his dad's house there was an uproar. His dad left Chris with Jen's mum and got dressed. At two o'clock in the morning he drove straight over to his ex-wife's house, stormed into the hallway, up to Chris's room and packed his son's bags.

I was exhausted listening to it. Jen then went into detail about the aftermath but I was too preoccupied to take it in. Only one fact interested me: that Chris Stoker was no longer an occasional visitor to my best friend's house. He was living there. I would see a lot more of him.

Jen left college early that afternoon, saying that she had to get home to help Chris sort out his new room.

Apparently there was furniture to move around, cupboards to clear, decorating to be planned. It was only after she'd gone that I realized that I hadn't mentioned the second love letter. There simply hadn't been space in Jen's conversation to fit it in. It didn't matter anyway, because the second letter felt more *private* than the first.

When I got home I found my mum sitting at the kitchen table with two piles of exercise books, one either side of her. She had her glasses on and was underlining something in red and tutting.

"Hi, love," she said, taking her glasses off and looking up at me. "Had a good day?"

"An absolutely brilliant day," I said, smiling.

FOUR

Chris had been living at his dad's house for almost two weeks when I received the next letter. I had seen glimpses of him a couple of times but he appeared to be busy, looking for another job, going back and forth to his mum's house for things that he needed. The row had subsided but everybody seemed to think it was best for Chris to stay with his dad for a while.

This suited me.

I found the letter when I came in from work. I was feeling tired after a long day at the supermarket but I snatched it off the hall table and took the stairs two at a time until I was in my bedroom. Then I opened it.

Dear Victoria,

I always wanted a college girlfriend. And now I've got you. I love you.

X X X X X

I plonked down on the bed and kicked my shoes off. Then I lay back and read it over and over. There were more handwritten kisses than before, some getting bigger at the end of the line. The message itself was sweet, jokey. *How many more?* I wondered. *How many blue envelopes would there be before something was said?*

Later, as I was about to leave for Jen's, I considered taking the letter with me. After a few moments' indecision I decided against it. I quite liked the idea of keeping it from Jen. My own secret romance.

Jen's mum, Cheryl, made some coffee and chatted. I nodded and replied but all the time I was wondering when Chris Stoker was going to appear. I could hear movement from upstairs, footsteps on the ceiling and doors opening and closing, but as of yet I hadn't seen him. Jen was spreading some cottage cheese on rice cakes, which she insisted was very nice. I was eating a Hobnob, nibbling at its edges, not really tasting it or paying attention to what I was doing.

"How's your mum?" Cheryl said, placing a cup of milky coffee in front of me. "Is she still working at St Mary's?"

"She's applying to be deputy head there," I said.

"Really?"

I nodded absent-mindedly, my ears picking up the sound of heavy footsteps coming down the stairs. A few moments later the kitchen door opened.

"Hi, Victoria," Chris said, noticing me immediately.

I smiled and then buried my nose in my coffee cup, taking a mouthful of lukewarm liquid. He went straight to the fridge, pulling the door open and taking out a carton of milk.

"What you doing up there? Sounds like a herd of elephants!" Jen said, giving him an affectionate hug.

"Just me," he said, pouring a glass of milk.

I watched as the two of them chatted with each other. They didn't look particularly alike. I found myself focusing on Chris. I'd known him for years, seen him dozens of times, but it was only recently that I'd started to look closely. He was taller than Jen but much thinner. His hair was dark brown and flicking over his ears as though he needed a haircut. His eyes were dark, looking out from behind rimless glasses, which he was always cleaning. His clothes always looked a bit wrinkled; his denims pale blue, his sweatshirts and shirts washed out, clean but full of creases, as if he was so busy he hadn't got round to ironing.

"When did you say Sam was coming down?" he asked Jen.

"Next weekend," she said, giving me a look of delight.

"I said I'd take him to a pub by Hampstead Heath."

"Not without me!" Jen said.

I'd forgotten that Sam was due a visit. I sighed inwardly. It usually meant that Jen was tied up for the whole weekend and I was left on my own.

"It's a blokes' thing," Chris said, with his hands in mid-air, playfully fending her off.

"Go on!" she said, putting her arm round his back. "We could go on Sunday afternoon. Vicky could come!"

I perked up.

"I suppose so," Chris said, looking over at me. "But you'll both have to buy me a drink."

"I think you should be buying them a drink," Cheryl said, soberly.

Chris left the room, nodding his head exaggeratedly, saying, *Yeah, yeah, what about equal rights and all that?* I watched as the door shut gently behind him and experienced this frisson of excitement which I tried to hide by gulping down my cold coffee. I was going to Hampstead Heath with him. I could hardly believe how easily it had been arranged. After a few minutes I heard his steps on the stairs again, and then he shouted *Bye!* and the front door banged. Neither Jen or Cheryl seemed to notice. Jen finished her rice cakes then got up and gestured for me to follow her. Cheryl gave a little wave as I went.

"Come and look at Chris's room," Jen said, going up the stairs in front of me.

It was the room that Chris had usually stayed in when he came to visit for weekends. Now it was much fuller altogether, with a stacking stereo on the floor and piles of books and CDs around the place. The desk that was usually quite empty now had a computer monitor and keyboard. I walked in and sat down in the desk chair. Jen flopped on to the bed, not caring that she was lying across some of Chris's clothes. Then she leaned across to the clock radio and flicked a switch so that the room was full of music.

It felt odd being there, as if I were trespassing. I hadn't minded in the past, when Chris was just Jen's half-brother. But now that I had feelings for him it felt altogether different.

When had that happened? That change in my feelings?

I could pinpoint it; eight weeks before, at Jen's mum and dad's anniversary party. It was a big do in a hall and Jen's mum had said I could stay over at their house. Even though it was a party for adults Jen was sure that there would be some lads there.

"One of my dad's friends has got two sons, and his boss, I've been to his house, he's got a son of seventeen. I know they're all coming. And Jason from next door!"

We weren't exactly over the moon about it. Sam lived too far away to come and none of the others were of much interest to us. But it was a party and there would be alcohol, and people to dance with, so we made ourselves look forward to it.

We spent ages getting ready, trying different outfits and make-up and listening to our favourite CDs. We played loud music and drank from a secret bottle of fizzy wine. Jen's mum and dad left early for the hall but we went later, not arriving until just before ten. We made an entrance, both slightly tipsy from the wine. The first person I saw was Jen's brother, Chris. He put his arms around each of our shoulders and led us towards a table in the corner where his dad and Jen's mum were sitting. We left our coats while Chris went to the bar and got us some drinks.

It was hot and dark in the hall and the music was louder than I'd thought it would be. I had to shout at Jen to make myself heard. She nodded enthusiastically at the things I said but I could tell she wasn't really listening. Her eyes were roving round the hall, and in minutes she dashed off towards a couple of lads who were standing talking together, cigarettes in hand.

I waited, thinking she would bring them over. I stood, feeling awkward, as she seemed to fall into easy conversation with them. I didn't know whether to follow her or not and I left it so long that it became too late anyway. She was firmly ensconced with the two lads. If I turned up then I would have been like an outsider. A moment later one of the lads gave a little wave and walked off, and when I looked back Jen was in a passionate clinch with the other.

I was flabbergasted. *What about Sam?* I wanted to say. How had it happened so quickly? Exactly what had she said that had led from a conversation to a series of deep and long passionate kisses? I felt isolated and for a minute I thought about getting my coat and going home. Then Chris Stoker was standing beside me, looking over at his sister.

"She doesn't waste her time," he said.

I shook my head, feeling faintly ludicrous, the kid who was left over when the teams were picked. Chris took my elbow and guided me to a quieter part of the hall, and we leaned up against a post and started to talk.

"How's college?" he said.

"Good. Different to school."

"Which A levels are you doing?" he asked.

He wasn't just being polite so I told him. He had done history, the same as me, so he asked me which exam board and we talked for a while about the syllabus and the coursework. When we'd exhausted that subject there was a moment's silence and I thought that he'd make an excuse, walk away, leave me on my own. Instead he started speaking about something completely different.

"Karen and me split up, did Jen tell you?"

I nodded and he proceeded to tell me about it. How they'd gone out for over a year. How she'd been the one who wanted to be serious, to be in a one-to-one relationship. He hadn't been ready to settle down but when they'd started to sleep together he'd known it was the real thing. And then, out of the blue, she'd said she wanted to be on her own.

I hardly heard the end of what he said because I was fixed on the bit about them sleeping together. He'd told me straight out, as though I was a close personal friend. It had a curious effect on me. The beginnings of a blush crept up my neck, but at the same time I had this stirring in my stomach, a silly fluttery feeling. The music had slowed down and the lights had almost gone out completely. There were just speckles of colour from a light rotating at the front of the hall. I wasn't sure if it was the fizzy wine or the heat or the thought of him in bed with a girl but I began to feel mildly giddy. I should have sat down but all of a sudden he was pulling me towards the dance floor.

I put my hands up to his shoulders but he pulled me closer and I ended up hugging him as we edged here and there among the crowd of slow dancers.

The music was too loud to bother speaking and

anyway I had no idea what I might say. All I knew was that his body was flattened against mine, my face buried in his shoulder, my breasts pushed into his chest. From time to time he moved his hand up and down my back, making my skin tingle and my stomach flip over.

Then the music ended and the lights came up suddenly and I found myself blinking a few times. Chris laughed at me, the bright lights glinting in his glasses, then he leaned over and gave me a quick peck on the cheek.

"Thanks for the dance, Victoria," he said.

There were speeches and toasts and within a few minutes Jen was back at my side telling me all about her experiences. I listened, shell-shocked, my eyes following Chris as he wandered off and disappeared into the crowd. I didn't see him again that night. Jen said he was going back to his mum's and was seeing his ex-girlfriend the next day to see if he could work things out with her. He never did.

In the eight weeks since the anniversary party I had seen him a number of times and he had been friendly but nothing more. Now I looked at his things on the floor of Jen's spare room and felt a mild exhilaration at having him so near, so handy, so accessible. Then there were the letters; the slim blue envelopes, my name carefully typed out in full, just the way that he enunciated it, *Victoria*.

Jen had stopped lying on his bed and was sitting up, looking restless.

"You're looking dreamy," she said to me.

"I was miles away," I said, although it was a lie. My thoughts were focused on things that were much closer to home. Her brother and his letters.

FIVE

There was a long queue at the checkout. Several people were looking exasperated but I was going as fast as I could. A young man was packing his items slowly, talking soothingly to a baby in a pushchair who was on the brink of being fractious. I looked at the clock. My break was due any minute. I was longing for it. In the distance I could see Mr Messenger, one of the supervisors, at his station, looking down at some papers. He had a Biro in his hand and was scratching his head with it. Beside him were a couple of women who had come on a later shift than mine. He was probably about to allocate tills to them. I was hoping one of them would take over from me so I could go and have a coffee.

It had been a long day.

The man with the baby was handing me his reward card. I swiped it through and waited while he peeled off some money. Looking round I noticed a familiar face coming up one of the aisles. It was Ricky Fairfax, the lad from college whom Jen thought would make a good boyfriend for me. I felt immediately irritated. I put my head down and started to feed the next lot of food items past the scanner. From time to time I looked up to see if he was anywhere near. I had this tension at the back of my neck which got worse when he came into view. Even though he hadn't looked in my direction and kept disappearing from my sight I was acutely aware that he was there and that he might see me and come over for a chat. After I'd totalled up for the next customer I was hugely relieved when a small grey-haired woman patted me on the shoulder and took over the till.

In the staff room I took my shoes off and put my feet up on the chair opposite. I rubbed my head against the back of the chair to ease the tightness that was there. I felt myself relaxing and then had this sweeping feeling of ridiculousness. What was wrong with me? Ricky Fairfax was just shopping in the supermarket and probably didn't even know that I worked there. How could I be so unkind as to try and avoid him when he wasn't even looking for me? It was all Jen's fault. Because she had suggested that he had written that first letter I had begun to feel awkward around him. I hadn't believed it then, and since the subsequent letters had arrived I was even more convinced. The letters were written in a more mature way. They were blunt and odd, almost ironic. But they were real, I was sure, the message in them, *I love you*, exaggerated as it was, was sincerely meant. That's why they couldn't have been written by a seventeen-year-old boy.

I pushed it all out of my mind and thought about the next day, the trip to Hampstead Heath. I still couldn't quite believe it and had been waiting all week for some disaster to happen and for it to be cancelled. Nothing bad had occurred, though, and I had sorted out my stuff ready for the trip, ironing and re-ironing my top and trousers and polishing my boots, almost as though I was going for some kind of job interview. I had also taken a light blue bra and pants set out of its cellophane wrapper and snipped the labels off, leaving it dangling over the back of a chair in my room. I was excited, I can't deny it.

Looking up I saw the staff-room door open and Mr Messenger, the supervisor, come into the room and walk purposefully towards me. I looked at my watch and only then realized that I'd over run my break time by more than five minutes. I stood up, immediately apologetic.

"Gosh, I'm sorry. I lost track of the time," I said.

A couple of the other part-time workers were standing behind Mr Messenger, smirking, enjoying my embarrassment. Mr Messenger didn't seem angry, though, which was a relief. He was in charge of the rotas for part-time workers and had been known to be unpleasant at times, quite bossy at others. One kid said he should have been a head of year at a school. I generally tried to keep on his good side, asking him frequently about his new baby and his wife.

"Pardon?" he said.

"I've taken longer than I should have. I'll make it up. . ."

He waved his hand dismissively.

"No, no," he said. "It's OK. We're not that busy. Stay and finish your tea. A few minutes here and there won't make much difference."

He looked as though he was about to turn away when

he seemed to remember something. He pulled a blue envelope from his pocket.

"Oh! This came for you. It's probably better to have mail sent to your home address rather than here. Things can get misplaced. . ."

I took the letter from his hand and was about to apologize again when Mr Messenger turned and walked away. The other kids, who had been watching, straightened up and gave him cheesy smiles as he passed. As soon as he left one of the girls came hurriedly towards me.

"Who's it from?" she said.

I shrugged my shoulders as if I didn't know. Then I put it in my overall pocket and went back out on to the shop floor. I was at my till station for almost three hours before I asked for a loo break. Once inside a cubicle, with trembling fingers, I pulled open the envelope.

Dear Victoria,
You brighten up my life. I love you.

X X X X X

There it was again. Just some words on a piece of paper, but they made my head go light and my skin tingle. I folded it up and spent the rest of my shift aware of it sitting heavily in my pocket, the words burning into me.

At the end of the day I picked up my coat and went home. I wanted to spend the evening having a long bath and then an early night so that I looked my best the next day. I didn't even bother to wait for a bus, I simply skipped along. I was happy. Why shouldn't I be? It wasn't just Jen who had some passion in her life, it was me as well. All I had to do was to wait for Chris to make the next move. Not another letter, I didn't mean that. I had to hold my breath and wait for a look, a smile, a touch. Then I would know for sure.

That was why the trip to Hampstead was so important.

SIX

Sam had grown a lot since the last time I'd seen him. He was taller than all of us and he'd broadened out, his chest solid and strong. Throughout the day he wore a Manchester United football shirt on top of his jumper and no coat.

He had a kind of satisfied look about him, as though he was very happy with his life. This had something to do with Jen, I was sure. She looked different when he was there; her hair bouncier, her face glowing. Sitting beside him on the sofa she looked smaller altogether. When she was with me I heard all the lurid details. She said that when her mum and dad were out of the way Sam was all over her, covering her with kisses and squeezing her ribcage so hard that she couldn't breathe. After that he tried gently worming his way into her blouse or undoing her jeans. The best thing, she told me in a whisper, was in the middle of the night, when her mum and dad were asleep. Sam crept into her bedroom and lay on top of her covers. She said these things in a scandalized tone of voice, but her eyes were glittering and I knew that she was loving every minute of it.

After having a drink in a smoky pub on the edge of Hampstead Heath the four of us decided to go for a walk. We started off cheerfully, Sam and Chris joking about football teams and me and Jen chatting aimlessly, most of our attention on the boys.

After a while we seemed to get lost. Chris had an *A to Z* of London but it was tiny and the map of the heath was the size of a postcard. There were no signs so we just kept walking, Jen laughing all the time at Chris, saying that he had a hopeless sense of direction and Chris telling her to *stick to cooking and having babies and leave the important stuff to men*.

After about an hour of wandering the mood began to dip. It was a chilly afternoon with a sharp wind. There was rain in the air, the sky looking heavy and the clouds a charcoal colour. Sam and Jen were walking behind, hand in hand, the wind pulling Jen's jacket to one side, her hair blowing wildly. Sam's red football shirt stood out against the greens and browns of the heath and he was rubbing his arms with the cold. I was trying to keep up with Chris, who was narrowing his eyes every time we came to a crossroads. After a while of walking aimlessly, being passed by runners and bike riders and even the odd family, we all stopped and looked at each other.

"I'm sure I recognize that pond over there," Chris said, tersely.

It was getting dark, the edges of the sky becoming shadowy. The pond he was pointing at was tiny, the water still, like soup, with just a couple of ducks who seemed to be moving through it with some effort. By the side there was a wooden structure with a seat that looked like an old bus shelter. There was no road, though, and no buses. I didn't recognize it at all.

The three of them got into a huddle around the *A to Z*, their voices sounding sharp and irritable. When the rain started I hunched my shoulders and stood feeling left out and useless. Sam was hugging himself, the sleeves of his jumper pulled over his hands, the nylon of his Manchester United shirt rippling in the wind.

"It's starting to rain," I said, lamely. Nobody looked round.

I focused on Chris, bent over the map book, his hair being blown about by the wind, his hand shielding his glasses from the rain. Then I thought of the letters sitting in my drawer, all four of them, neat blue envelopes with matching paper. Was it really Chris who had sent them? Suddenly, freezing cold, in the gloom of the deserted heath, I wasn't sure. The rain was splashing down by then, no longer a light spray but heavy and cold, each drop drumming into my forehead. I felt miserable. I closed my eyes for a few moments. I'd been wrong. Chris hadn't sent me any letters. He had no feelings for me at all.

A hand on my arm made me look up. Chris had grabbed my sleeve and was pulling me along. Jen and Sam were up in front, heading for the shelter that was by the side of the pond. I began to run along with Chris, my hand falling into his, his grasp firm and warm. My spirits lifted, my worries about the letters flying out behind me. When we got to the wooden shelter Jen and Sam were laughing, Sam looking down at his football shirt which was dotted with rain.

"You should have a coat on!" Jen said.

"I didn't know we were going cross country. I thought this was London! All shops and cars and pubs."

The two of them sat down on the bench in one corner of the shelter. Sam had his arm around Jen and she immediately lifted her feet off the ground and put her legs across him. There was no space between them, they seemed to wind round each other.

"What are we going to do?" Jen said. "It's getting dark!"

She was right. From inside the shelter we could see just how much the daylight had faded.

"I'll look after you," Sam said, nuzzling his face into Jen's hair.

"We'll let the rain stop," Chris said. "The street lights will come on soon, and that'll give us some direction. We should be able to find a way off the heath."

I must have looked worried.

"Don't worry," he said, putting his arm around my shoulder for a few moments, "no one's ever gone missing or starved to death on Hampstead Heath."

"Anyone ever froze to death?" Sam said, visibly shivering.

"I'll keep you warm," Jen said.

With that she started to kiss him full on the mouth, her hands in his hair. I only watched for a minute then I had to turn away, coughing slightly to cover my awkwardness. I found myself face to face with Chris who was also looking at the couple.

"Kissing cousins!" he said, lightly.

I nodded, stamping my feet on the ground, pushing my hands as far into my pockets as they would go.

"Come and sit over here," he said, pointing to the other side of the shelter.

We sat down side by side and looked out at the darkening sky as the rain sliced through the air. I had my back turned to Jen and Sam and I put the palms of my hands together and slotted them between my knees to keep them warm.

"You're cold, aren't you?" he said.

"A bit," I said, my voice croaking with nervousness.

"Here," he said, leaning back against the wood of the shelter, "I'll warm you up."

He put his arm round my shoulder and used his other hand to pull his coat across so that it covered part of my knees. I felt awkward at first but I warmed up and began to relax, my neck easing. I could feel his warm breath on the side of my face and I watched as he got his mobile out of his pocket and turned it on so that it gave off a green light. Using his thumb he typed in a message and then sent it. I wondered if it was for his ex-girlfriend, Karen.

A groaning sound from behind made me look round. The other end of the shelter was almost dark and Jen and Sam were still kissing, their faces twisting and turning with fervour. I could just see that Jen's eyes were closed and she'd opened her coat and Sam's hand was underneath her jumper. I stared for a moment, unable to look away. In the gloom of the late afternoon I could see the white of her midriff as his hand rubbed at her breast. It gave me an odd feeling: I should have been embarrassed or disgusted – instead I had this yearning, this desire to be there, in that corner.

I don't really know where I got the courage from but when I turned back, and saw Chris also looking at his sister and her boyfriend, I put my hand up to his face and pulled it down so that his lips were close, and then I kissed him.

He was startled for a moment, I could tell. But then, as I pushed my mouth harder on to his, I felt his arm closing round my shoulder, pulling me towards him, his lips moving across mine, his fingers back and forward across my neck. I let my head go limp as he seemed to take over. My eyes were closed and I lost myself, no longer aware of my surroundings. I felt him gasping for breath in the dark as his hand dropped and wriggled its way in between the buttons on my jacket. I helped him. I undid it and felt a swooning sensation as his fingers stroked back and forward across my chest. I smiled then, thinking of the blue bra and matching pants.

How long did it go on for? Seconds? Minutes? It seemed like hours. And then it stopped suddenly.

"Look!"

Sam's voice broke the silence. I opened my eyes and could see, in the distance, the glow of a row of street lights that had just snapped on. Sam and Jen were standing up, Sam fidgeting, moving around, rubbing his hands together. Chris was sitting forward, away from me, and I could feel the cold air surrounding me, forcing its way inside my coat, all along my neck. Jen was looking out of the shelter and didn't seem too interested in us. She'd obviously been so entangled with Sam that she hadn't noticed her best friend and her brother in a clinch.

"It's stopped raining," she said. "We can head for those lights and get back to the tube."

We walked across the dark heath, keeping to the paths as much as we could. Jen and Sam had their arms round each other but Chris was a couple of metres in front of me, his *A to Z* in his hand even though it was too dark to see the page. From time to time he looked round to make sure we were all behind him. He seemed completely absorbed in finding his way, so I just followed, my head still spinning with the excitement of what had happened.

When we found the lights at the edge of the heath and walked on to the tarmac of the road everyone cheered up. The underground wasn't far away and Chris was chatting with Sam as we went into the brightly lit station and got our train. We were all sitting in individual seats, side by side, looking at our reflections in the opposite window. For once Sam and Jen were separate and we all looked a bit dazed.

On the street, outside the station, Sam and Jen walked off, Jen saying that she would see me in college the next day. Chris waited a moment until the pair were further up the road.

"You all right?" he said, stepping towards me, his hands in his pockets.

I looked up at him and he lowered his head and kissed me lightly on the forehead.

"I better go," he said, gesturing after Jen and Sam who were further up the road.

"OK," I said.

I wasn't disappointed. I was keen to get off and be on my own. I wanted to go over the afternoon, to think about it, to recreate it in my mind.

"I'll see you later," he said, and gave me a little smile.

Then he was gone, his back disappearing up the road.

SEVEN

Jen told me about the party first thing Monday morning. It was to be the following Saturday, the day before Chris's nineteenth birthday. We spent our first free lesson poring over the details of it.

"Just think," she said. "Chris's friends. All those lads in my house!"

"What about Sam?" I said, with mock outrage.

"He's in Norfolk."

We were sitting on a bench in the courtyard outside the student common room, eating out of small plastic boxes. I had a cheese and pickle roll, 280 calories, and Jen had a banana and two crisprolls, 150 calories. We were shivering with cold but the common room was full of loud boys larking around.

The common room was a dingy place anyway. It sat on the edge of the college, out of sight, out of mind; two classrooms knocked through and filled with battered armchairs. It was just beyond the science block and it took about ten minutes to walk there from our usual classrooms. The courtyard where we were sitting was the smokers' area so it was littered with dog-ends and empty cigarette packets. There was even rubbish in the surrounding shrubs and trees, some beer cans and fast-food boxes. The bench we were sitting on was the only nice thing about the place and that was only empty because it was so early in the day.

From where we were we could see the edge of the college, a low brick wall and beyond it the road, still full up with queues of traffic tailing back from the rush hour.

"I thought you and Sam were really close," I said, remembering the weekend and Jen's passion for her cousin.

"We are! But he's not here, and it's not as if I'm going to run off with someone! It's just a bit of fun!"

"Oh," I said.

It wasn't my idea of a relationship, but who was I to talk. I hadn't yet had a serious attachment to anyone. Until then. On Sunday, during a busy spell when I was reorganizing my room, I'd got my love letters out of the drawer and looked at them again. When I replaced them it was in a kind of flippant way. There probably wouldn't be any more, I thought, with mild regret, because now we'd moved on. There'd been a kiss, more than a kiss. There would be another move; a meeting, a talk, an embrace, anything would do. I was just waiting. Now there was to be a party.

"You could invite someone," Jen said, peeling her banana and holding it upright, savouring the moment before she bit into it.

I didn't answer. I was half hoping that Chris might have said something or that she, herself, had seen us kissing on Saturday. I was wondering whether to tell her or not when I noticed, with some consternation, that

Ricky Fairfax and a couple of his mates were weaving through the traffic and heading for the college. I stood up quickly.

"We should go," I said, glancing at my watch.

Jen looked surprised, her mouth full of banana. "What's the hurry?" she mumbled.

Ricky Fairfax and his mates passed by and went into the common room. He had barely given a nod in our direction and I felt foolish. We left anyway.

It was a busy week and the days flew by.

I didn't spend every moment daydreaming about Chris Stoker. He had occupied my thoughts a lot, I can't deny it, especially since the anniversary party. I had spent hours remembering all the different times that I'd been in his company, from the early days when I'd first known Jen and we were two little boffins and he was a kid with heavy glasses. I didn't see much of him then; three, maybe four times a year if I happened to be at Jen's house when it was his turn to stay with his dad.

As each of the blue letters arrived I began to pore over every meeting we had had in recent years, when he was visiting Jen and talking about his college courses or his plans for university or his girlfriend, Karen, who was studying art. I treated these memories like a set of photographs, looking over and over them. I began to hypothesize. What if me and Chris got together? What if we became a real couple? What if we slept together? Not just one awkward fumbling night, but regularly, as though it was the most natural thing in the world?

I worried about it as well. What if he didn't have the courage to make a move? The letters were confident and to the point. *I love you*, they said, but I was sure that that wasn't what they meant. *I fancy you* was more likely, *I want to go out with you, I want to go to bed with you.* "Love" was a funny word. We used it all the time for all sorts of people. Maybe it was just a sort of exaggerated way of saying *I like you. Take notice of me.*

And then I thought, what if I got embarrassed and gave off the wrong message? If I was too shy and he thought I was rejecting him? Sometimes I completely lost confidence. What if he hadn't sent the letters at all? If I had quite literally misread the whole thing? The face of Ricky Fairfax always came into my head at this point and I brushed the image away as though it were an irritating insect.

Since the weekend, since the kiss, I hadn't needed to think too much about it. Something had happened. We were a sort of couple. I began to feel more relaxed. I had space to think of other things. I had work to do. There were a couple of assignments due in before Christmas and I needed to get myself up to date. I went to the library and the computer suite, and took reams of notes in the relevant lessons. I worked late in the evening and used my dad's laptop to catch up on my work. During the day I let a lot of Jen's chatter go over the top of my head, and I even told her to shush a number of times so that I could concentrate.

Whenever I began to get anxious, thinking about

Chris or the letters or the party, I just made myself remember the kiss by the pond on Hampstead Heath. That was it. The sign that told me I'd been right about my feelings, about his flirting, about the letters. I was calm. For the first time I was quietly confident, so much so that I made up my mind to tell Jen.

By the end of the week I had handed in first drafts of three assignments. I had made plans for a fourth and tidied up and reorganized my folders. I'd found books in the library that were useful and downloaded material from websites. I felt as though I was on top of things.

On Friday afternoon, on the way home from college, Jen and I went into the local shopping centre. I had money to buy something to wear. She was going to help me choose. After browsing in all the main shops I found a red dress that I liked. I held it out from the rail and Jen's eyebrows shot up.

It was short and tight and had a low neckline. It was quite unlike anything I had ever owned.

"You like that?" Jen said.

I nodded, trying to look confident, my insides quivering. It was more scarlet than red. Definitely aimed at someone older, someone with a different lifestyle. Not me at all, and yet I pictured myself in it. I wanted it. I could feel the money burning a hole in my purse.

"I'll just try it on," I said in an offhand way as if I didn't care.

"You've got no chest. It'll make you look too skinny."

"I'll just have a look and see."

Jen looked astonished. She shrugged her shoulders and followed me into the cubicle. I felt her disapproval as I slipped my clothes off and stepped into the dress, carefully pulling it over my hips and upwards, my hands slipping through the straps. There wasn't much room in the tiny cubicle but I stood back and looked into the mirror.

I looked like a completely different person. I liked it. I had the wrong bra on and my hair was a mess but the dress made me look older, my shoulders and arms looking shapely, my legs, usually hidden under jeans and trousers, feeling cool, exposed. I needed different shoes, I knew, but it was right, I felt it. I gave Jen a sideways look.

"You'll hardly get much wear out of it," she said, "but it does look nice."

"I'm having it," I said, letting it drop on to the floor and stepping out of it and back into my jeans.

"You'll need a red bra," Jen said, with a weary air, as though she was only going along with it because she had to.

"I've got one," I said. "A matching set that I bought a while ago."

"You never told me!"

"You don't tell me every time you buy a pair of knickers!"

"I do!"

I laughed as I handed my money over to the cashier. Later, when we were on the bus, Jen told me about Ricky

Fairfax and how he'd asked her about me at least half a dozen times, quizzing her as to whether or not I was going out with anyone.

"What's so wrong with him? He's nice-looking!" she said.

"I know he is. I just don't fancy him."

"He's getting a car, he told me. As soon as he passes his test."

"Why don't you go out with him?"

"I've got a boyfriend!"

"Well, so have I!"

There, I'd said it. Like laying out a winning hand in cards. I threw it down in front of her.

"What boyfriend? Who?" she demanded.

"I think me and Chris are getting it together," I said, my voice croaking a little. I found myself clutching at the bag which held the red dress, the tissue inside crinkling under my touch.

"Chris who?" she said.

I looked at her with dismay.

"Your brother, Chris!"

I was disappointed. I had wanted her to twig immediately, as if it was something she'd suspected all along.

"Don't be silly," she said, and laughed.

"I mean it," I said, placing the dress bag flat on my lap and smoothing it out.

"Chris is too old for you! Anyway he's got a girlfriend!"

"He's finished with Karen."

"That's what he says. He always goes back to her. How can you be his girlfriend? He would have said something to me."

"On Saturday, up at Hampstead Heath—" I started, my confidence slipping in the face of Jen's incredulity.

"So you and Chris had a snog! That doesn't mean anything."

"I don't know how you can say that," I said.

The word *snog* disgusted me. All sorts of people used it, I knew. It suited some situations, I supposed. Couples at parties getting together for an hour, snogging madly in a dark corner then drifting off to see if there was anyone better on the loose. It made the physical act of kissing sound like fast food; something you devoured like a burger and chips. I didn't like it one bit.

"I thought you were only messing about," Jen said. "You can't take Chris too seriously about stuff like that. . ."

I gave a tight nod. I could have said something about the letters but I decided not to. All week I'd been thrilled about what had happened to me and Chris, and in a few moments Jen had reduced it to something casual. A quick snog, like a piece of bubblegum chewed and then spat out.

"Never mind about Chris. Think of all the other lads who will be there!"

That was it. Even though Jen was mad about Sam she was always willing to grab the opportunity of being with someone else, even if it was only for a quick fumble. Sam was her number one, but she never turned anyone else down. She was hungry for boys. I was different.

When we got off the bus she gave me a quick hug.

"We'll get you someone really nice," she said, and skipped off up the road.

I walked along with the dress bag shoved in my rucksack, my feet feeling heavy. When I got home the house was in darkness. I switched on the hall light and saw the letter on the mat. A blue envelope, just like the others. I was hardly breathing as I dropped my rucksack on the floor and bent down to pick it up. With the front door still flapping open behind me I opened it. The paper was the same, thick and expensive; the message direct and clear.

Dear Victoria,
  I can't wait to see you tomorrow. I love you.

X X X X X

I turned the envelope over. This time it simply had my name on, with no address. The sender had dropped it in by hand. I felt this rush of pleasure. If I had returned a few moments earlier I might have seen him, might have been able to take the letter, literally, by hand.

Tomorrow. Chris's party. Jen was wrong. She had to be wrong. What other explanation was there?

EIGHT

I had to work the late shift at the supermarket so I knew I wouldn't get to the party until after eleven. I still woke up early on Saturday even though I could have slept past lunch time if I'd wanted.

My mum was in her study for most of the morning, doing her job application. I drifted in and out of the room and she showed me the letter she was writing. Two pages of closely typed reasons why she should have the job as a deputy head in the school where she was currently working. *That'll show your dad*, she'd said jokingly, her hand twitching on the mouse, her eyes sliding back to the screen.

My dad was around, reading the papers, listening to music, watching the pre-match football programmes on the telly. At midday he made me a bacon sandwich with brown sauce (at least 600 calories) and a mug of steaming hot tea.

I left for the supermarket early, walking instead of getting the bus. I was going straight from work to Chris's party so I'd packed a towel, underwear, my red dress and toiletries, as well as the present that I'd bought and wrapped in gold tissue paper. When I got to work I put them all carefully in my locker and put my overall on. Mrs Lister, one of the supervisors, handed me my wage slip and I stuck it in my bag and went out into the store. At four o'clock I settled down on a stool next to a till and tried to smile at all the weary Saturday-afternoon shoppers. Mr Messenger passed by and told me what time my break was going to be. He was wearing a dark jacket and had a new badge on with the words *Paul Messenger, Assistant Manager*. He was looking more stern than usual and I promptly punched my code into the till and started work.

There couldn't be many more boring jobs than being on the checkout. Especially on a Saturday when the customers came through in an unbroken stream, one giant stack of shopping after the other. Sometimes I timed myself to see how many customers I could do in an hour, other times I counted the *types* of people who came through: mums, dads, teens, grannies, students, office workers and even, occasionally, nuns and priests. Mostly I just put myself on autopilot, a weak smile on my lips, and let my mind wander. That Saturday I didn't seem to be able to do any of these things and the minutes dripped by, one at a time. Just after my break, when I'd completed half my shift, time seemed to stand still. The minute hand of the clock simply didn't move, it looked as though it had been painted in that position. Twenty minutes past seven. It seemed like twenty-four hours had passed since I'd first sat down on the stool and turned my key in the cash register.

By the time it was twenty to ten I thought I was going

to explode with impatience. The store was almost empty, a few customers drifting by now and then, mostly youngish people buying bottles of drink and packs of beer. Mr Messenger came round with the time sheets for the following week.

"You might as well go," he said.

"Thanks!" I said, surprised. He was renowned for making people stay till the last minute of their shift, especially the lads.

I closed down my till and signed off. Mr Messenger was looking tired, rubbing his eyebrow with the heel of his hand. I felt this stab of sympathy for him, especially as he had let me pack up early.

"How's your baby?" I said. "Emily, that's her name, isn't it?"

"You remembered." He smiled. "She's lovely. Doesn't sleep much, but she's lovely."

"You should bring her in one day," I shouted, walking away from the till.

"I will!"

His voice disappeared into the background as I skipped the last few steps out of the store and into the staff area. I got my stuff out of my locker and went into the ladies' washroom and shower. I locked the door and stripped off.

The shower was scalding hot and I had to wait for a few minutes for the cold to filter through. The jets of water pierced through me, making me tingle, lifting my spirits. I closed my eyes and looked upwards into the gushing flow, letting it soak through me, waking up from the long, tedious afternoon and evening. Afterwards, I wrapped my towel around me and sat on the tiled floor of the washroom. I felt warmed through and watched as the steam slowly disappeared before my eyes. Then I got up and looked in the mirror. I used the dryer for my hair and then started to get dressed. I took my time. It was only ten fifteen and I was in no rush.

When I put the dress on I had a queasy moment. Had I been right to buy it? Jen's lack of enthusiasm had dented my confidence. I hadn't even shown it to my mum and dad, just shoved it in my wardrobe and then packed it up to take to work. I stood back. It was certainly a transformation. No longer a geeky schoolgirl, but a confident young woman. The red bra straps were showing through but that didn't matter. I sighed, sprinkled some glitter on my shoulders and sprayed some perfume on.

My hair was almost dry. I put lipstick on and smiled at myself. The gap in my teeth looked huge but I shrugged my shoulders. It was no different from normal. I gave an exaggerated smile and clapped my hands. That was it! Enough pampering. I was ready to go.

I cleared up my stuff and opened the door. After being in the shower room for so long the staff room seemed downright cold. Fortunately there was no one there so I could leave without anyone noticing how dressed up I was. I put everything into my locker and pulled my coat out. I was just about to put it on when I heard the staff door opening and shutting. I turned round and saw Mr Messenger standing there.

"Victoria!" he said, looking at me with surprise.

"I'm going out, so I thought I'd get changed. Save me going home."

I didn't really know why I was explaining it to him. I suppose it was because he'd been so nice about letting me go.

"Anywhere nice?" he said, pleasantly.

"To a party. Hence the dress," I said, gesturing.

He looked at the dress and raised his eyebrows. When he didn't speak I began to feel a bit uncomfortable.

"It's a birthday party," I said. "My boyfriend's."

It was only half a lie. It didn't matter though. Let him think I had a boyfriend. Why not?

"Someone from college?" he said, walking towards the cupboards where the kettle and the tea things were.

"No. . ."

I really would have liked to have gone there and then, but I'd started talking to him and I just couldn't stop halfway through a conversation.

"It's my friend's brother, actually. He's nineteen!"

I put my coat on and put the small gold package into one of my pockets.

"Are you getting a taxi?" he said. "It's a cold night."

"No, she only lives a few minutes away. Henderson Street, just by the swimming pool."

"I know it. I live down that way myself. Well, have a good time," he said.

I walked away, glancing over to check that I'd closed my locker. He had his back to me, fiddling with the kettle.

"Goodnight."

"Bye," he said, without turning round.

I walked out, through the deserted aisles of the supermarket, my shoes clipping along the floor, the lining of my coat moving silkily against my bare shoulders and arms. I felt free. I felt exhilarated.

A cold wind hit me outside the doors but I pulled my coat around me for warmth, my hands in my pockets, one of them touching the shiny paper that Chris's present was wrapped in. Then I walked smartly off in the direction of the party.

NINE

It was noisy and smoky and I couldn't see Chris Stoker anywhere. After a few moments of standing in the hallway with my coat on, Jen came rushing through and gave me a hug. She looked flushed, as though she'd had her own secret bottle of fizzy wine. It was as though she hadn't seen me for months.

"I thought you were never coming!" she said.

I was surprised to see Cheryl, her mum, in the doorway of the kitchen, holding a glass of wine and chatting to a couple of young lads. I nodded at her and followed Jen as she dragged me upstairs to her room. She was wearing jeans and a sparkly top with some silver shoes. She looked really pretty and I suddenly felt completely overdressed, holding the neck of my coat in a bunch at my throat.

"Come on, let's see you!" she said, standing back.

I slipped the coat off feeling cold and exposed.

"Wow! I have to admit it does look good."

But I didn't feel that good. There were goose pimples on my arms and my legs felt cold. I wished I'd just put my regular clothes on. I smoothed the fabric down and looked in the mirror. Perhaps Jen had been right. I was too flat-chested for a low-cut dress. I sighed and straightened my back. It was too late to worry about it.

"Let's go and get a drink," Jen said, not noticing my discomfort.

I followed her along the landing, taking a quick look in Chris's room where the bed seemed to be covered in coats. As we went downstairs the noise got louder, the beat of the music thrusting beneath a sea of chatter.

"How come your mum's here?" I shouted, stepping in between people and heading for the kitchen.

"Dad's here as well. They weren't going to leave us in the house on our own. Anyway Chris wanted them. This is a proper grown-up party, after all."

I nodded. That was a relief. The couple of parties that Jen and I had gone to while at school were very furtive affairs. Hidden bottles of wine and beer and the lights off while someone's mum and dad had gone out to the cinema. Lots of writhing couples and music so loud it felt like my eardrums were splitting.

Jen got us a small bottle of beer each. Her dad waved cheerfully at me. We were allowed to drink which felt good. We went into the living room and Jen pointed out all the people that she knew. She had to shout in my ear as she put names to the various couples who were standing around the room. Among them were Chris's mum and stepdad, who were chatting happily to some young girls.

Just then Chris came in, another lad following close behind.

"You all right, sis?" he said, putting his arm round Jen. "Not getting too drunk?"

He was looking around the room nodding at various

people. Then his eye settled on me. For a moment he looked puzzled, as if he didn't know who I was.

"Victoria! You look nice."

His words had an exaggerated feel to them but his eyes were looking me up and down in a way that made me feel very odd. I swigged back my beer and looked away with embarrassment.

"This is Gerry," Chris said, gesturing at his friend, a big lad with almost no hair and what looked like a knitted jumper on.

"Hi," I said, as Chris put his hand on my arm and his mouth close to my ear.

"You look terrific!" he said. "You'll have to dance with me later. Could you chat to Gerry for a while? He doesn't know anyone."

I nodded and he squeezed my arm and went off. I felt immediately relaxed. We were going to dance later. Jen was staring into space, her head nodding to the beat of the music. I turned to Gerry and asked him how he knew Chris.

"We worked in a burger bar. 'Food operatives', we were called. It was a right laugh. . ."

Then he proceeded to tell me several stories about burgers: *There's the fifteen-second rule. If it drops on the floor and lays there for more than fifteen seconds you can't serve it to the customers.*

"Goodness. . ."

I started to speak but he continued at a pace. I nodded a few times, trying to look as though I was listening, but after a while I'd had enough. Jen wasn't helping, she seemed to be in a daydream. At that moment the door opened and a couple of lads from college came in. I smiled with relief. I could make my excuses and leave. But then Ricky Fairfax followed them in and I had this flutter of irritation. Gerry was still talking about something called *Food Hygiene Regulations* and I turned round and looked at Jen with annoyance. Why had she invited Ricky? She saw my face and leaned over towards me, speaking in my ear.

"He asked me if he could come. I couldn't very well say no!"

"Yes, you could!" I hissed, angrily.

Gerry slowed down and ended with the words *toxic gas. . .*

"Gerry," I said, brightly, "have you met Jen? She's Chris's sister and is very interested in food."

It was a mean thing to say but I left them to it. I brushed past the college boys with hardly a word and pointedly ignored Ricky Fairfax. I went out to the kitchen and got another bottle of beer, and stood by the fridge pretending to listen to two lads talking about cars. After a third bottle and all the information I needed about *high insurance premiums* I walked off, picked up another beer, and found myself standing by Jen's mum, Cheryl.

"You look lovely, tonight, Vicky," she said.

"Thanks," I said, my eye scanning the room to see if Chris had come in.

"Red suits you," she said. "Did you come on your own? I thought you might bring a boyfriend."

"No," I said.

"Ah! Well, we'll have to find someone for you," she said.

I was about to tell her not to bother when some new people came into the kitchen and her face lit up.

"Excuse me, Vicky," she said, moving away from me.

My beer was only half-finished but I put it down and picked up a glass of white wine. Looking round I came face to face with Ricky Fairfax, who was also getting a drink.

"Hi, Victoria."

I didn't speak at first, just gave a non-committal nod. He kept trying.

"Did you get all your assignments in? Only I saw you in the library."

It was only an enquiry but it annoyed me. He'd seen me in the library. What was he doing? Spying on me? I didn't answer, just slumped against the wall, the effect of the quick beers making me feel a little light-headed. I remembered then that I'd hardly eaten since lunch time, just biscuits with my tea at break.

"You look nice," he said.

I looked closely at him. He was smiling, his eyebrows raised in a hopeful way as if he was expecting something good to happen. He had amazing teeth, straight and even like an American film star. This depressed me for some reason. I let my tongue flick in and out of the gap in my own teeth.

"That dress suits you," he tried again.

"I know," I said, with great patience. "That's why I bought it."

I caught the hint of a frown on his face and then it cleared.

"See you later," he said and walked off.

I didn't feel bad. I just felt relieved. I looked down and saw that my wine glass was empty, so I went back to the drinks table and filled it up. The room had got darker, I was sure, because it was harder to see who was around. I scanned the faces, looking for Chris, but he wasn't there. I was still feeling a little light-headed and I edged through the tightly knit drinkers and stood at the living-room door. He wasn't there either, but I saw Jen and Gerry dancing closely together. Jen's head was on Gerry's shoulder. His hands were moving up and down her back. I shook my head. How could she?

I stood for a minute, completely aimless. Then I remembered the gift I had brought which was still in my coat pocket. I went upstairs to Jen's room and got Chris's present from my coat. Walking back out on to the landing I saw Chris, in his room, opening and closing his drawers. I decided to give him his present, out of sight of the other partygoers. Why not?

I coughed lightly and he turned round.

"Happy birthday," I said, holding out the package.

He looked a little distracted but even so his face broke into a smile.

"You shouldn't!" he said and took the gift.

I walked into his room and plonked myself on the bed, feeling the mound of coats underneath me. He tore the paper off roughly and then smiled at the CD.

"Thanks, Victoria. I really like this band."

I knew that. Jen had told me. His pleasure gave me a bolt of confidence and I stood up and walked over to him.

"And a birthday kiss," I said, on tiptoes, my face turned upwards to him.

He gave a little laugh but lowered his head. The kiss was brief, just a touch on the lips, then he pulled back. He gave me an odd look, his eyes flicking down, across my chest. I didn't want to stop. I put my hands up to his face and pulled him towards me. He kissed me again, harder this time, his hand stroking along my shoulder, pushing the strap from my dress so that it slipped down and hung on my arm.

He became more certain, his arms encircling me. I seemed to be walking backwards, towards the bed. His mouth was turning from side to side, his hand sliding back and forward across the silky material of my dress. My neck seemed floppy and my head felt heavy. When I couldn't go any further I slowly sat down, drawing him with me. I wanted to arch back, to lie down. It seemed the most natural thing in the world. I wanted to pull him on top of me but underneath I felt the buttons and the lumpiness of the coats digging into my back.

Then he stopped and I had a moment of dull panic. He had changed his mind. He was going to go downstairs, to the party, and leave me alone. I closed my eyes, not wanting to look. All I heard was the sound of the door shutting and a key being turned. Then he returned, without a word, and sat on the bed beside me, pulling me up so that he could move the coats over. When there was a space I lay back. I opened my mouth to speak. I wanted to tell him how I felt but he put his finger on his lips as though I was a little girl. He took his glasses off, laid them on the bedside cabinet, leaned over, and kissed me again.

In moments he was lying down, his breath heavy and urgent, his hand underneath the fabric of my dress, his fingers pressing into my skin. I felt this aching in my ribs and my stomach. It was rash, it was stupid, but I couldn't have stopped it. I could hear the noise of the party, the music from the floor below, odd voices squealing or laughing. When he started to undo the back of my dress I wanted to help him. I sat up to do it but was stopped by a banging sound, an urgent knocking on the door of the room. Chris looked round, a dazed expression on his face, as if he couldn't quite remember where he was.

"Chris! Chris!"

It was Jen's voice.

"Are you in there? Chris, open up. It's important."

"Wait. . ." he said, clearing his throat.

"What are you doing in there? What's going on?" Jen was getting impatient.

He leaned over and retrieved his glasses, putting them

on quickly, pushing them roughly up his nose. He stood up and held his hands out to me. I gripped them and he pulled me up. I thought, this is it. This is when he tells Jen about us. *This is the beginning*. In silence he led me towards the door. I was only seconds away from seeing Jen's face. I felt light, as if I were walking on air. I scooped up the strap of my dress and smoothed down the fabric.

But when we got to the door of the room he directed me to the side and put his finger on his lips. I was puzzled but I stepped away, which was what he seemed to want. He let go of my hand and gave me a gentle shove so that I was on the edge of the door. I was confused but I didn't say anything as he turned the key and pulled the door towards him.

"Hi," he said, just opening it a few centimetres.

"What you doing?" Jen demanded.

I realized then that I was behind the door. Hidden behind it. So that Jen couldn't see me.

"I had a headache. I was just taking five minutes out," Chris said.

"Karen's here."

"What? You're kidding."

He sounded genuinely surprised. I honestly believed that he hadn't expected his ex-girlfriend to turn up.

"She wants to see you! She's a bit tearful!"

"Well. . ."

Chris gave a half-look in my direction and I felt this heavy feeling in my chest.

"I'll be down in a minute. You go on, I'll follow. . ." he said and then closed the door.

"I'm sorry, Victoria," he started to say and I felt this swooning feeling of relief. He was going to go down and get rid of her. It was an inconvenience, that was all. She was tearful so he had to go.

"Thing is, her and me . . . we've been talking about getting back together. I didn't think she would come. I had no idea."

How wrong could I have been?

I leaned against the wall. I hadn't moved from the place where he'd hidden me. I felt smaller somehow, as if in those moments I'd shrunk. He, on the other hand, seemed taller, his shoulders square, his head held high. The news about his ex-girlfriend had boosted him.

"But what about us?" I said, weakly, gesturing towards the bed.

He looked around as though he might see something there.

"Victoria, you're a lovely girl. I really like you."

"And the letters. . ." I said.

The blue envelopes with their messages of love. What about them?

"Letters?" he said, kindly, realizing at long last that I was upset. "What letters?"

He looked at me with a quizzical expression, then he glanced at his watch. There was just a hint of impatience.

"I'll go down and speak to Karen. Then I'll come back up. We can talk. All right?"

I nodded. What else could I say?

"I'll be back. A few minutes. Ten minutes? OK?"

I watched him go and the door close behind him. I waited. Even though I knew he wouldn't be back.

TEN

I waited for almost forty minutes.

The music from the party was pouring in through the open door and from time to time I saw figures passing on their way to the toilet. A couple of people came in and sorted through for coats and one young girl asked me if I was all right. I told her I had a headache. Otherwise I was completely alone watching the figures on the digital clock. One minute it was 01:05. A few minutes later it was 01:30. Time was racing away from me, every minute that flew past making it more unlikely that Chris would return.

I sat on the bed among the coats like a wilting flower. My red dress seemed garish and my naked shoulders felt cold and bony. I let my tongue play around with the gap between my teeth, pushing hard as though I might be able to break through. I didn't cry, I didn't even feel particularly upset. I just felt ridiculous.

He hadn't sent the letters and he had no real interest in me. He had a girlfriend who he wanted to be with. I was someone to flirt with, pass the time with. When something important happened I was hidden behind the door. I was just a snog. All that stuff on the bed, all that passion and urgency. It was nothing more than fast food.

I was supposed to be staying the night with Jen but I

wanted to go downstairs and slip out. I stood up and walked out of Chris's bedroom and straight across to Jen's room to get my coat. Then I went to the bathroom on the other side of the landing. I splashed my face with water and looked in the mirror. I looked awful, dark circles under my eyes, my skin like plastic, expressionless. I decided not to put my coat on, afraid that it would draw too much attention with people wanting to say goodbye. I folded it up and hung it over my arm. I was about to go out when I heard some voices coming up the stairs. I ducked back in and then realized that it was Jen speaking. Looking out I saw her and Gerry going into her bedroom, and the door closing behind them.

Like sister, like brother, I thought bitterly.

I went downstairs and found myself smiling at people, raising my eyebrows, nodding and saying thanks as they let me squeeze through. At the bottom I paused for a moment and looked sideways into the living room. Chris Stoker was dancing with a tall blonde girl. They were sandwiched together, her head twisted slightly so that it fitted into the crook of his neck. His arms were wrapped around her and his eyes were closed.

True love. Perhaps it was.

I turned to go and saw Ricky Fairfax there. I remembered the letters. Had he sent them? I didn't know and I didn't care. He gave me a half-smile and I gave a little wooden nod and walked round him and out of the front door of the house.

The cold air hit me like a smack. It woke me up and I

quickly unfolded my coat and put it on. The sound of the party was muffled but I could still hear the music. The street, on the other hand, was still and quiet, most of the house lights were off, the front doors tightly shut, the cars tucked up by the pavement. It was almost two o'clock and I had to get home. I only lived about ten minutes' walk away but it meant going through dark streets on my own. I pulled my coat tightly round me and went out of the gate.

A car came out of nowhere and pulled up a few doors down. The low beat of music came from inside it. When the sound stopped and the lights went off a couple of lads got out. They were talking loudly, their voices booming out in the quiet street. I was surprised to see that one of them was Sam. He noticed me immediately.

"Vick," he said, cheerfully.

He was wearing a coat this time and carrying two four-packs of beer. So was his friend.

"I thought you couldn't come?" I said.

"Donny's dad's car," he said, pointing at his friend. "Two hours it's taken us, but still. Anything for my Jenny."

He was looking delighted with himself. His friend less so, placing the cans on the ground and rubbing his hands together.

"She's inside. . ." I said but couldn't go on.

Jen was inside with Gerry, up in her room.

"Are you going home?"

"I've had enough," I said. "I've been at work all day and I'm tired."

"What about the birthday boy? I thought you and him. . ."

Sam didn't continue.

"No," I said, "That was just . . . a bit of a laugh."

I felt a lump in my throat. How simple it would have been. Me and Chris. Jen and Sam. Why couldn't that have happened? Why did Karen have to show up? Another hour and things might have been different. Another ten minutes and things would have been different.

He nodded. Behind him his friend was getting impatient.

"I'd better be off. Give Jen a nice surprise."

"She's in her room," I said and he turned and walked off.

Another ten minutes in Chris's room and it might have been a lot worse. Me, lying on his bed, my dress like crushed petals underneath me, him getting up, throwing his clothes on so that he could rush downstairs to see his ex-girlfriend.

Sam was up to the gate, his friend hurrying him on. He turned for a moment and gave me a little wave. I could have stopped him. I could have gone back into the party, slipped upstairs and warned Jen that Sam was coming. I could have knocked urgently on her door the way she had knocked on Chris's. Then silly Gerry could have hidden the way I did. Me and Gerry. We were just pastimes. Maybe it was right that Sam would see what Jen was like.

I walked off along the street, wrapping my coat tightly round me, hugging it to my chest, my head down, just taking one step after another.

ELEVEN

I got to college late on Monday. Classes had already started so I slipped into my lesson nodding an apology to the teacher. Jen was in another class so I knew that for thirty minutes or so I was not going to bump into her. I got my pad out and put a pen into my hand and sat looking as though I was taking notes. In fact I was just writing gibberish. Printing my name over and over again.

No one paid any attention to me.

As my pen moved on the page I thought about Jen and what she would say to me when I saw her. How many times, over the previous day, had I wished I had not told Sam where Jen was. It was a mean thing to do, and it had sat in my chest like a heavy stone.

I got up late on Sunday, sleeping until midday. I woke up with a dry mouth and a heavy head. For the first few minutes my mind was blank and I didn't think of the previous evening. I felt physically tired and hungover but I didn't have any bad thoughts. And then, sitting up, stretching my arms out, hearing my bones crack, I saw my red dress lying untidily across my bedside chair and I remembered the scene in Chris's bedroom. Him talking to Jen about his real girlfriend and me tucked behind the door out of sight. It gave me a cringing feeling. If only I had left then, just walked out. If only I hadn't stood, cow-eyed, and asked him about the letters. *Letters?* he had said, and it had all become clear in a second. He didn't have those feelings for me. The kissing and stuff was just something to do. I pulled myself out of bed, picked up the red dress and shoved it in the bottom of my wardrobe.

My mum and dad were out for most of the day so there were no probing questions about why I hadn't stayed over at Jen's. The house was empty and it gave me time to wallow in my unhappiness. Strangely, though, I was not broken-hearted about Chris Stoker. I was embarrassed. I was ashamed. I was mortified. But I was not broken-hearted. I felt much worse about what I had done to Jen. I thought of ringing her, but was afraid that Chris would answer.

Then there were the letters. I got them out and laid them on the bed in front of me. How could I have thought that Chris had sent them? The words *I love you* stood out from each of them. Just looking at them irritated me. What had previously given me pleasure now filled me with shame. I thought of Ricky Fairfax and his perfect teeth and his friendly smile. Had he sent them? Had he bought a special set of matching envelopes and notepaper and composed these tiny bullets of emotion?

I scooped them up went downstairs to the kitchen. I took the pages over to the gas hob. I lit one of the rings and took the first letter by its corner and held it over the flame. When it caught light I held it for a moment before dropping it into the sink. I followed with the others until there was just a mess of black ashes. It gave me a feeling of satisfaction. The business with Jen and Sam couldn't be solved so easily, though.

In college, writing nonsense on my notepad, I wondered whether I would ever be able to sort things out with Jen. A rumble of chairs from around me told me that the lesson was over. I packed up my stuff and went to my tutor room.

I was the first to arrive so I took one of the seats by the window, looking out at a grey sky and drizzling rain that blurred the edges of the cars that were parked alongside the classroom block. There were several students standing around, their coats fastened up, their shoulders hunched against the wet, their fingers holding on to cigarettes. The classroom door opened and shut a few times but Jen didn't come in. I wondered if she was late and I looked beyond the cars towards the college gates but there was no sign of her running along the pavement. Just a man in a long leather overcoat, standing with his back to the college, probably waiting for a bus.

She came in suddenly and I was taken aback. She didn't scowl or pout, her expression was neutral. Ricky Fairfax followed close behind, deep in conversation with some other kid. Jen sat down a couple of seats away. It was only a step or two but it felt like she was at the other side of the room. I got up and shifted chairs until I was beside her. She stiffened for a second, then I could almost see her shrinking into her chair, her shoulders becoming rounder, her chin dipping into her neck.

"Jen, I'm so sorry," I said, "I was going to ring you. . ."

She seemed to square up as I spoke, shifting her bottom about on her seat.

"You told Sam!"

"I didn't mean to. . ."

That wasn't the truth but I didn't know what else to say. I could hear my tutor's voice in the back of my head languidly calling out people's names and the answers: *Yes. Yeah. Here. Here. Yep. That's me. Yeah.* . .

"I was in a bit of a state," I said. "About Chris. . ."

"Chris and Karen?" She looked incredulous and answered me in a loud whisper, "I told you he would go to go back to her. You were upset about that and you took it out on me!"

"I'm so sorry. What happened with Sam?"

"Sam went straight back to Norfolk. But not until he'd hit Gerry."

"Oh no!"

I remembered Gerry with the shaved head and funny jumper.

"He split his lip. Me and my dad had to take him to casualty. He had two stitches. We had to wait for four hours!"

I registered the door of the classroom opening and someone coming in. I glanced round, glad of some excuse to turn away from Jen. It was one of the admin staff, the big grey-haired lady who worked on reception. She had a pile of leaflets in her hand. As I turned back I found myself face to face with Ricky Fairfax. His eyes met mine and then he looked away. Jen was fiddling about in her bag. A second later she produced a bag of crisps, salt and vinegar flavour. She used her fingers to pull it open and then pulled out a crisp and held it in front of her.

"Sam's finished with me now. And it's all your fault!"

She popped the crisp into her mouth. I wanted to say *280 calories* but it wasn't the time.

"Just because you had a stupid crush on my brother! I end up being dumped!"

I had some responsibility, that was true, but it wasn't all my fault. She'd conveniently forgotten the bit about taking Gerry up to her room.

"I'm sorry," I said, in spite of a growing sense of annoyance.

She was pouting. She didn't look particularly satisfied, as though she wanted me to put up more of a fight. I was about to speak when I heard Bob call out my name. The grey-haired receptionist was leaving. Bob was holding something in his hand. A letter. A blue envelope.

My heart sank. I did not want another letter. I looked angrily at Ricky Fairfax. His head was bent over the desk and he was looking closely at a magazine.

I got up from my seat and walked over to Bob. I plucked the letter from his hand without saying a word. I glanced down at it, sighing loudly as though it was guaranteed bad news. It was the same as all the others, except for the words BY HAND in the corner. I forced my finger into the envelope, tearing the top of it. With impatience I pulled out the carefully folded sheet of blue paper. I found myself grinding my teeth, giving Ricky Fairfax a last angry look before I read the contents.

Dear Victoria,

You looked so nice in your red dress. I want to be your boyfriend. I love you.

X X X X X X X X X X

I vaguely heard Jen's chair scrape as I took the words in, *your red dress*. I turned to Ricky Fairfax just as he was closing his magazine.

"Did you send this?" I said, my voice louder than I intended. A number of the other kids stopped what they were doing.

"What?" he said, in a friendly tone.

"This letter? Are you sending these to me? Are you?"

I stepped closer to him, holding the letter up in my hand like a flag. He was looking puzzled, his eyes moving from the piece of paper to me and then to the kids around. His expression changed to one of complete incomprehension.

"Are you sending these to me?" I demanded.

But even as I said it I knew he wasn't the one. Something about his silence, his look of bewilderment, the way he did a kind of double take, giving the kids around a sideways look as though I was completely barking mad.

78

"I just wondered. . ."

My voice faded and I went back to my seat. I only noticed then that Jen had gone, and so had most of the other kids. Ricky walked out in a little group of boys, their heads tightly together, a snigger or two coming from them. In moments I was completely alone in the classroom, the love letter hanging limply in my hand. I knew I had to pull myself together. I'd been hasty, silly, but sitting there only made things look worse. I stood up and was unhooking my bag from the chair when I glanced out of the window. I stopped what I was doing and focused on the college gates. The man in the leather coat was still there. I'd thought he was waiting for a bus, but there were a couple behind him standing at the stop, passengers stepping into them. He'd had his back to me before, but now he was facing me.

I knew straight away who he was. He saw me looking and gave a little wave, just a tiny one, his hand in front of his chin. He was smiling and looked a lot different from usual, the leather coat making him look like a spy out of a film. Mr Messenger, my supervisor from work. He was outside my college standing waving and smiling at me. As if he had some reason to be there. I lifted up the blue paper and envelope, above the neat address the words, BY HAND.

This time he had delivered the love letter himself.

TWELVE

I should have gone straight out and confronted him. Marched up to the man, the letter in my hand, and demanded to know what he was playing at. He had a wife and a baby. He was nearly thirty. I wasn't remotely interested in him.

But I didn't.

I went into one of the cubicles in the Ladies, pulled the seat cover down and sat on it for almost an hour. My mind racing, I only half heard the comings and goings of female students, the doors opening and closing, the toilets flushing, the taps gushing, the hot driers blowing, the frippery of a dozen conversations.

If anyone had asked I would have said I was just biding my time, trying to decide how to deal with what was an embarrassing situation. In reality, though, I was hiding. Waiting until the man in the leather coat had walked away from the front of the college. Waiting until the coast was clear and I could slip out of the gates and go home.

I looked at the letter with disgust. Wasn't it enough that it hadn't come from Chris Stoker? Wasn't it bad enough that I had made a fool of myself, throwing myself at him, falling out with my best friend, accusing Ricky Fairfax of being the sender?

How much more punishment was I going to have?

I remembered then that Paul Messenger had actually given me one of the letters himself. *It's probably better to have mail sent to your home address,* he'd said, sounding concerned. I felt nauseous thinking of him with his badge and his clipboard, pretending to be helpful.

Surely there was a funny side to it, wasn't there? If Jen knew she would make me laugh about it. We would take the mickey out of him, call him a saddo, snigger at his attempts to be romantic, feel sorry for his wife and baby. Jen wasn't around, though, and I was on my own.

I waited until the bell went for lunch when there were hundreds of students walking out of the front gate. I hid myself in the middle of them, feeling great trepidation in case Paul Messenger was there, waiting for me. I jumped on the first bus going in the direction of home. Once indoors I busied myself making a cup of tea, just delaying the moment when I would have to sit down and face up to the fact that I was in an awkward position, and I would have to do something about it.

I wasn't due to go into work until the following Saturday, so there was no real need to do anything until then. I didn't feel comforted by this fact. It was Monday and I had four days to get through. There might even be another letter. I pictured the postman pausing at the front door and felt a kind of mild panic. If I did nothing for four days would Mr Messenger take that as a sign of disinterest, as I hoped, or would he interpret it as coyness? Either way I would have to face him, stand in front of him and refer somehow to his feelings for me. The whole situation seemed completely unreal. I pushed it from my mind, took my bag up to my room and tried to do some work. I laid all my folders out and proceeded to tidy them up, even though it wasn't necessary. I got some notes out of my history file and started a rough plan of an essay. After two or three attempts when my mind kept wandering I gave up, lay back on my bed and aimed the remote at the television. I must have watched on and off for a couple of hours. The programmes gave me something to focus on and I was grateful. Every time the credits rolled I felt this mounting anxiety, remembering what had happened, why I was in such a pathetic state.

At four-ish I heard the front door bang and my mum's voice calling up the stairs. That's when I thought about telling her, asking her advice. It came to me in a flash and I wondered why I hadn't considered it before. I was reminded suddenly of that time when I was eleven or twelve and Jordan Hill, a boy from my class, had started to take an interest in me. We were no more than children, really. I was tiny, my chest as flat as an ironing board and my periods still a thing of the future. Jordan's dad had died some years before and he lived on his own with his mum, just round the corner from us. We'd walked to school and back together and we'd gone to the park a couple of times. It was before I got really close to Jen. These meetings certainly weren't dates. There was nothing physical, we were simply too young.

One day there was a knock at the door and my dad said, *It's your boyfriend!* And I felt this acute embarrassment. I started to avoid Jordan after that, setting off early for school and staying in the library to do my homework. But he was always hanging around the street, looking up at my house. I told my mum in the end and she went round to see his mum and that was it. I hardly saw him after that.

My mum had been so matter-of-fact about it all. As if it was the sort of thing that happened all the time. She'd rung up Jordan's mum and made an arrangement to go round there. It had sounded to me like making an appointment at the dentist. She sorted it out for me in the way she did everything: efficiently.

I went downstairs clutching the letter. In the kitchen I found her stooped over her laptop, her hair hanging in her eyes. She was using her nails to tap loudly on the wooden table.

"What's up?" I said, surprised to see her looking dishevelled.

"I've just lost a mail merge," she said. "It took me days to get all the data on and somehow, I'm not sure exactly how, I can't find any of it. I can't have saved it before I left work."

"Maybe Dad'll know how to get it back."

"I'm sure he will," she said, gloomily.

"Do you want a cup of tea?" I said, the letter still in my hand.

"Not at the moment. I've got to find this. It might be

better if I did it in the study. On top of that I've got this interview on Friday. There's a presentation to prepare. *Which Way Forward for Eleven-to-Sixteen Education?* I've got ten minutes in which to persuade them to give me the job."

She stood up and snapped the lid of her laptop closed.

"You can get your own tea, can't you, love?"

I listened to her trudging upstairs, grumbling under her breath. I couldn't tell her about it at that moment. She was too busy, too harassed. I made a decision. I couldn't wait for four days. I had to go and see him then, at that minute, to put him straight. It was the only way I was going to be able to get the whole thing off my mind.

It was late afternoon and the supermarket was busy. Mr Messenger was at his station, surrounded by a number of women in overalls. He had a clipboard in front of him and was directing each of the cashiers to a till. One by one they walked off, leaving him alone. I paused for a minute, standing back behind the magazine rack, not knowing what to do, what on earth I was going to say.

He was wearing his usual work clothes, dark trousers and a white shirt with a company tie. Although I couldn't see it from where I was I knew he'd have his new badge on, *Paul Messenger, Assistant Manager*. He was young to be a manager, only late twenties, someone had said. He'd started working in the supermarket when he left school and been there ever since, working his way up. He was slim, although he had a small round stomach that sat above the waistband of his trousers. His hair was receding on the top so that his scalp was visible. At the same time he always looked as though he needed a shave, his skin tinged with darkness as though he was in the early stages of growing a beard. He wasn't unpleasant to look at, but he seemed older than his years.

I watched as he picked up the receiver from the wall phone behind him and started to talk, nodding, using his pen to scratch at something on his head. His eyes were sweeping across the till area, resting on each one and then moving on. Then he noticed me. I had no choice. I had to face him.

"Hello, Victoria," he said, when I walked up to him.

"Mr Messenger. . ." I said, clearing my throat.

"You're not on today, are you?"

He was making a show of looking at his staff lists. He knew I wasn't working that afternoon.

"No . . . I just came because I wanted to have a talk. . ."

"Ah. . ." he said, laying the clipboard down. "Anything wrong?"

"It's about this," I said, pulling the letter out of my back pocket.

He looked down at it, his expression bland. It was a piece of folded blue paper, curled at the edges. He didn't react in any way. It might have been a till receipt or a leaflet for a new type of yogurt. After a few moments' silence, he spoke softly.

"I'm just finishing here," he said. "We could talk in the conference room? In about ten minutes? Why don't you get a coffee and I'll see you in there?"

I walked briskly away, down the aisle, past the rows of olive oil, honey and jam, the loaves of bread and dog food. I didn't get a drink. I went straight to the conference room, pulled out one of the chairs from the big table and sat down. I unfolded the letter and laid it on the surface of the table. I made myself sit up straight, as though I was about to be interviewed for a job.

He came in a couple of minutes later, a pleasant expression on his face.

"Victoria," he said. "There you are."

He pulled the next but one chair out from where I was sitting. He turned it sideways so that he was facing me. He sat in a relaxed position, his legs spread and his hands loosely clasped. I turned towards him.

"You got my letters," he said, giving me a cheery smile.

"Yes. I. . ."

"I wondered when you would say something." He leaned towards me, his expression soft.

"The thing is. . ." I said.

"I know it must seem strange," he went on. "Someone like me having feelings for someone so young, but. . ."

"I'm really flattered, you know . . . I never thought. . ."

"You're such a sweet, pretty thing."

"It's just that . . . I never for one minute thought that you. . ."

My words were floating away from me, meaningless and ineffectual. He was sitting very still, his eyes on me. I could smell a sweet aftershave and I could see that he'd loosened his tie and undone the top button of his shirt. There was hair curling out from his chest and it made me feel deeply uncomfortable. I looked away.

"You're married, Mr Messenger," I said, firmly.

He sat upright when I said this, a dim smile flickering across his face as though he'd expected this comment and was ready for it. He linked his hand into the free chair that was between us and hooked it away.

"I am married. But only in law. My wife and me, we don't have a proper marriage. There's no love. She got pregnant, you see. I did the right thing. I married her for the sake of the baby, but it hasn't worked out."

"But your baby?"

"Don't misunderstand me, Victoria. I love my daughter but my marriage is over. We're together at the moment but that's only until we've sorted the finances out."

He was leaning towards me, his face concentrated, his mouth slightly open. I didn't know what to say to him. It was not a situation I had ever, in my wildest dreams, imagined or desired. He must have taken my silence for some sort of assent because he reached across and put his hand on my knee.

I stood up, grabbing the letter off the table.

"Mr Messenger, I'm sorry about your marriage but you must stop right now. I am . . . I cannot be interested in you. You're older than me, you have a baby. You must not send me any more letters."

"But I care for you," he said.

"But even if you were free, even then I couldn't get involved with you. I have a boyfriend already. You remember? I told you the other night. My best friend's brother? The one whose party it was?"

The words had an effect. He sat back, stiffly.

"But I love you, Victoria."

This was what I had wanted to hear for so many weeks. Words that I had wanted Chris Stoker to whisper to me. Now they had a different effect. A sense of dread settled on me like an unwelcome hand on my shoulder.

"Mr Messenger," I said, firmly, "Chris and I are serious. I'm sorry but you and I cannot have any kind of relationship."

He didn't answer.

"I must go," I said.

He stood up, fastened the button at the top of his shirt and began to fiddle with his tie.

"I'm sorry." I shrugged my shoulders.

"It's OK. You get off. Don't worry about me. I won't send you any more letters."

For a moment I felt this flood of sympathy for him. I wanted to put my hand out and pat him and tell him that it would be all right. He had drawn back, though, so it would have meant me walking towards him, and I didn't want to do that.

"Like I said. I'm really sorry. Maybe you and your wife could sort your problems out?"

He didn't speak so I turned and walked purposefully away, taking a deep breath as I left the conference room. Going out into the supermarket I half walked, half ran along the aisles. I didn't look back until I got to the outside doors. There was no sign of him, so I felt this surge of relief. Perhaps it was going to be all right. He'd said he wouldn't write to me any more. Most probably it had been a period of personal unhappiness for him and he'd simply latched on to me as a sort of substitute love. He was almost certainly embarrassed about it, maybe regretting that he'd been so forward in telling me how he felt. By the time I went into work on the following Saturday it would all be forgotten about. Walking along the road I was hit by the full situation. Wasn't Mr Messenger's infatuation with me simply a mirror image of my feelings for Chris Stoker? The circumstances were different, but when all that was stripped away, wasn't it just the case that he wanted me and I wanted Chris?

It was over. I took the blue letter out of my pocket and threw it into a nearby bin. Unrequited love. It happened all the time. People got over it. So would Paul Messenger.

THIRTEEN

Things began to look up. Jen sat beside me at tutor group on Wednesday. She asked me what lesson I had next even though she must have known my timetable off by heart. On Thursday she pulled out a blueberry muffin.

"Don't tell me," she said. "A zillion calories!"

"I'll halve it with you," I offered, even though I didn't feel much like eating.

On Friday she was even more like her old self.

"Sam rang!" she said, pulling a chair out excitedly and sitting down. "I'm going up to Norfolk tomorrow! Just for the day. I'm getting a coach."

Even the mention of Sam's name made me feel guilty. It must have been written all over my face because Jen noticed it and put her hand on my arm.

"Actually, he sounds keener than ever. Maybe it did him good to see me snogging someone else!"

That was typical of Jen. She was putting a positive gloss on the whole thing.

"I'm sorry," I said.

"Forget it. I hadn't realized how upset you were about Chris!" She rolled her eyes. "He's a real heartbreaker."

There was a faint hint of admiration in her voice. I shrugged. Let her feel proud of him. He hadn't broken my heart, just bruised my pride.

"We were all a bit drunk that night. The best thing you can do is come over tonight. Show him you don't care a jot!"

It was Jen's way of making up. I wanted to hug her. While the tutor was calling the register I found myself looking at my friend. She was so relaxed, so comfortable. She found it easy to get on with people – boys, girls, adults, anyone. That's why she was never short of a boyfriend and that's why we'd had such a long friendship. The only thing she couldn't control was her weight, and it niggled away at her. On the other hand there was me, as thin as a pin but riddled with anxiety. I thought of Paul Messenger, more nervous even than I was, reduced to sending anonymous letters to a girl who was a dozen years younger than him. It was on the tip of my tongue to tell Jen the whole sorry story. It meant explaining to her about the letters, though, and how I'd thought they'd come from Chris, and I wasn't ready for that. Maybe sometime later, when her brother was just a distant memory.

"Come over about seven," Jen said, as we split off to go to our lessons.

When I got home there were celebrations. Loud music was coming through the speakers in the kitchen and my mum was sitting with her feet up on the table, looking pleased with herself. She had been appointed deputy head of her school and was sipping from a glass of champagne that my dad had just poured for her. She was looking flushed and happy and my dad was jiggling up and down to the beat of the music. I gave her a kiss and left them to it.

Meeting Chris Stoker wasn't half as awkward as I thought it would be. On the way to Jen's I picked up a takeaway pizza. Chris answered the door, which I was quite grateful for, because it meant I had to speak to him immediately.

"Want some pizza?" I said, presenting it to him. "Baked-bean special," I added.

"You're kidding," he said, taken aback.

"Yes, I am," I said and walked past him towards the kitchen where Jen was sitting.

We divided the pizza up and ate it round the table. Chris chatted about his plans to move back home. He'd made it up with his stepdad and was going to return to his mum's house. I suspected his move back home had as much to do with him getting back with Karen as anything else.

"How's Karen?" I said, breezily.

"OK. We're just going to take it step by step. See how we go on," he said, looking a little shamefaced.

"That's sensible."

I was amazed at myself for being so detached. It was as if all that feeling, all that passion, had just floated away. There I was, just the week before, willing to do anything to be with Chris, and now he was just a lad with glasses and hair that was just a bit too long. What had happened to all those feelings I had been carrying round with me?

At the time they seemed to fill me up, to possess me, almost. Now they had gone, as if blown away by a puff of wind.

"Anyone want this last bit of pizza?" Chris said.

Later, in Jen's room, we talked about Ricky Fairfax.

"I shouldn't have invited him without telling you but he really likes you. I just thought. . ."

"He's a nice lad, but. . ."

"But there's no sizzle?" Jen said.

"When I see him I don't have any feelings. . ."

"Inside? In your guts?"

"Anywhere."

"I do know what you mean. When I see Sam I just want to push myself up against him, to get my hands inside his shirt."

"Yeah, but you feel like that with most lads!"

"No, I don't!"

I raised my eyebrows.

"Well, some lads."

"That Gerry? From the party? The most boring food operative on the planet?"

"He didn't look so bad in the dark."

"He had no hair!"

We were laughing, but it made me think of the party again and me telling Sam that Jen was in her bedroom.

"When Sam came in . . . to your bedroom. . . Were you, what were you doing?"

"Just kissing. Gerry had other ideas, but honestly I was passing time with him."

"Yeah, four hours in casualty!"

"It was a night to remember. A few lessons learned."

Jen said it seriously. I didn't speak but she was right. I had certainly learned an important lesson.

It was pouring with rain so I rang my dad and he said he'd pick me up about ten. I left Jen selecting an outfit to wear for her trip to Norfolk the next day. I shouted goodbye to Chris but there was no answer so I assumed he had gone out. I put my coat on and stood at Jen's living-room window waiting for my dad's car to pull up. I was feeling good, pleased that Jen and I had put the previous weekend behind us and that there'd been no real harm done.

I pulled back the net curtain and looked out on to the street, the rain falling in straight lines, illuminated in places by the streetlights. A couple of cars splashed by and two kids on bikes were cycling through the downpour. It wasn't the sort of night to be out and I was glad that my dad was coming to get me. I looked further along for signs of a car approaching and I noticed that someone was standing on the pavement holding a dog on a lead. I stood for a couple of minutes watching as the man stayed in the same position, not appearing to notice the rain pounding down around him. He was wearing some kind of anorak with the hood up but he had no umbrella and was turning from time to time to look up the road. Like me, he was probably waiting for a lift.

I swivelled away from the window for a moment,

gazing idly round Jen's living room. When I turned back I saw that the man was still standing there, only now he'd let his hood fall back off his head. The rain was crashing down and yet he was letting himself get drenched. Even the dog seemed unhappy, pacing up and down, its ears flat, its tail low and unmoving.

Then I realized who it was. Paul Messenger, in the rain, like a statue, looking in my direction. I was momentarily startled. I stood very still, peering through the window at this man who I could now see wasn't just standing anywhere. He was positioned so that he was staring straight at the front of Jen's house, his sights on the window where I was standing looking out, waiting for my dad.

Irritation buzzed through me. What was he doing there? Why was he standing so pathetically in the pouring rain? I almost called out to Jen so that she would come and look but he started to shuffle about a bit and I thought he was going to walk off. I made my way quickly out of Jen's house and into the rain, screwing my eyes up to see him, pulling my collar up around my neck. What on earth was he doing? Why was he there? Had he seen me go into Jen's and waited? The thought was too absurd. I'd been in there for over two hours. I felt the rain slapping into my face and realized that he had seen me coming out and walking towards him. He was smiling. This made me angry. Was he *following* me? Was that why he was standing outside Jen's?

"What are you doing here?" I said, loudly.

His face grew serious.

"I live round here," he said, pleasantly.

The rain was bouncing off his shoulders and he didn't seem to notice. My hair was flat and wet and there were droplets running down my forehead.

"Are you following me?" I demanded.

"I live round here," he said, his face dropping, looking hurt. "Twenty Margaret Road, if you don't believe me."

From behind I could hear a car approaching. I glanced round and saw that it was my dad.

"But why are you standing here? In the pouring rain," I said.

"I wasn't standing here in the pouring rain. I was walking my dog."

The car pulled up behind me and a horn sounded.

"Is that for you?" he said.

I turned to look at the car and waved at my dad, and when I turned back he had walked off, without a backward glance, the dog trotting happily at his ankles.

"Who was that?" my dad said, as I got into the car.

My coat was soaked and I could feel it through the layers of clothes I had on.

"No one," I said, unhappily.

FOURTEEN

I got to work early the next day intending to see Paul Messenger and straighten things out with him. I got changed into my overalls and went out on to the shop floor to see if I could catch him before the shift started. The supervisor's desk was empty, though, and so I asked one of the other checkout women where he was.

"I haven't got a clue," she said, looking fed-up.

I hung around with a couple of other part-time workers waiting to be allocated to a checkout. I looked around the store at the Christmas decorations. They'd been around for weeks but now that it was December they seemed to have grown, bloomed overnight, and were bursting out of every available place. There were cheery posters advertising turkeys and Christmas pudding and cut-out Father Christmases standing at the corners of aisles. The edges of the windows were sprayed with fake snow so that we looked like a Victorian grocery shop. It didn't make me feel at all festive. I was too busy looking for Mr Messenger, peering down aisles expecting to see him rushing to tell us which till to open up.

"I wonder where Mr Messenger is?" I said to one of the lads.

He shrugged and yawned as Mrs Lister appeared with the day's schedules. She took a kind of roll-call and then sent people off to their checkouts. When she got to me I asked her where he was.

"He's in a meeting all morning," she said, rolling her eyes. "So, I've been promoted for a few hours."

I walked towards my till, feeling sorely disgruntled. I wanted to find out why he had been there the previous evening. He had said he was walking his dog, but I had seen him with my own eyes standing in the rain staring across at Jen's house. Had he followed me there and waited until I came out? The very idea made me feel shivery.

The morning was busy, with an uninterrupted queue of shoppers waiting impatiently for me to filter them through. It was raining hard and there was a strong wind blowing in gusts so that the rain was hitting the storefront windows like a shower of tiny pebbles. The customers on the next till were grumbling because a man's card had been refused and his shopping was sitting in plastic bags in a kind of limbo while Mrs Lister tried to sort it out. Finally, it was time for my break, and I went to the staff canteen and had some tea and a roll.

It was odd not to see Paul Messenger. While I drank my tea I thought back over the months that I had worked at the supermarket. He was always around. When I first started he had personally shown me the ropes, trained me how to use the till, taken me for a tour of the giant store. After a few weeks he had taken me into the conference room and talked to me to make sure I was happy. He often stopped and had a little chat with me, asking about my college course and my studies. That was how I'd found out about his wife and his new baby. He was friendly. I had thought that was normal; even though I knew how some of the other part-timers, particularly the lads, found him overbearing.

At the end of my break I went to one of the other tills and relieved a lad called Arif, whom I'd known in school. A loud boy with a ring through his eyebrow.

"How would I find out where a member of staff lived?" I said.

"Ask me," he said, cockily. "I know where everyone lives!"

"Mr Messenger?" I said, sceptically.

"What do you want to know that for?" he said with a wicked grin.

"Oh, never mind," I said, realizing I shouldn't have asked. I should have kept my thoughts to myself.

"You don't *like* him, do you?"

"I said, it doesn't matter."

"Hang on," he said, ignoring me, "he lives near Darran."

He dashed off along the checkouts and spoke to a red-faced boy who was packing goods in carrier bags. They both laughed and Darran turned and looked in my direction. I plonked myself down on to the till seat with a feeling of exasperation. Why on earth had I asked Arif? Now he would be gossiping about me. I punched in my code on the till and gave the customer a half-smile. Then Arif was at my shoulder.

"Margaret Road. Darran lives further down. He don't know the number."

"I said it didn't matter!" I hissed.

I did know the number that Paul Messenger lived at. Number twenty.

I only saw him once all afternoon and then it was from a distance when he was talking to someone on the delicatessen counter. When it was time for me to go I got my coat and walked out the back of the shop, through the staff car park. It had stopped raining but there was a sharp, damp chill in the air. I hurried on, looking along the lines of cars. I was still hoping to see him. I had been feeling awful all day and as the afternoon wore on something became clear in my head. I would have to leave the job. I couldn't sit there feeling like that week after week.

I found him sitting in a red hatchback car, fiddling with his seat belt. I put my arm up to wave, hoping to stop him. His car moved slowly out of its parking space just as I reached it. He saw me and seemed to stay very still for a minute, holding on to the steering wheel, as if he were pausing at the lights and just about to zoom off. I walked to the driver's window and after a few seconds he leaned back and the window opened.

"Mr Messenger," I said.

"What can I do for you, Victoria?"

I saw the baby seat in the back of the car and suddenly felt very silly. Was I overreacting to all this? This was a married man with a baby. An older, grown-up man.

Someone who had a good job, who was in charge of people. Was it all a bit of silliness that, when all was said and done, amounted to nothing?

"About last night. . ." I said.

I was about to go on and apologize. To say I'd jumped to conclusions. After all he'd steered clear of me all day, avoided me, almost. He looked at his watch and then spoke, as if he was in a hurry and couldn't waste a minute.

"I can't help the way I feel about you, Victoria."

This threw me into confusion. He had meant to be there, to be standing on the corner of a street in the pouring rain waiting for me. He wasn't going to deny it.

"You followed me?"

"I wanted to see the boyfriend."

He said it bluntly, his fingers tapping on the wheel. I found myself avoiding his intense stare, looking at the passenger seat where there was a baby's bib and a packet of disposable nappies. Part of me wanted to laugh.

"Boyfriend?"

"I wanted to see him for myself. Like I said, I can't help my feelings."

Then the window slid up and he busied himself with the controls. After a moment he moved off and left me standing there, in the car park, the freezing air nibbling away at the skin on my face. I watched him disappear out of the exit and I knew then and there that I never wanted to see him again. Never.

FIFTEEN

First thing Sunday morning I wrote out my letter of resignation. Officially I should have worked the following Saturday to give them some notice, but I couldn't face it. I said I would go in during the week and return my uniform and pick up my things.

I'd thought about it long and hard the previous evening. I hadn't bothered to ring Jen because I knew she'd be on her way back from Norfolk. I'd thought of telling my mum but she and my dad left early to drive over to some friends for dinner. In any case I was reluctant to explain it to her. I couldn't be sure that she would have wanted me to leave the job. She might have wanted to make a big fuss and I wasn't ready for that. I just wanted to get away from him.

So I got one of my old DVDs out, something I'd watched a dozen times before, and slotted it into the machine. I didn't feel much like eating but I got a chilled meal from the fridge and heated it up. In the fridge door was an open bottle of white wine. I took a large glass and sat down in front of the television.

It was only eight thirty in the morning when I put my letter into the envelope. The store didn't open until ten on a Sunday so I had no choice but to wait. My mum and dad were still asleep and the house was silent except for the occasional clank of one of the radiators. I held the letter in my hand and it felt strangely weighted. It was just a flimsy white envelope with the words *Personnel Manager* written on it, but it felt curiously solid, its corners sharp and its edges straight. I sat it on my bedside table, slanted against the radio clock. The whole thing had started with a blue letter written on expensive notepaper and now it would end with a cheap white one.

I heard the phone ringing. In the quiet of the house the ring tone sounded impatient and seemed to get louder as it went on. I ran downstairs and picked up the receiver before the answerphone clicked on. It was Jen and she was upset.

"What's wrong?" I said.

"I've just come from the hospital. It's Chris."

She was openly crying and I could hear someone's voice in the background.

"What's wrong?" I said. "What's happened?"

"Chris was hurt. He nearly lost his eye. Oh, Vicky, it's terrible. He looks terrible."

And then she started crying again. At that point another voice came on and Jen's sobs receded into the background.

"Vicky? It's Cheryl here." Her mum's voice was crisp and business-like. "Poor Chris is in hospital. He was attacked late last night, mugged or something, we're not quite sure. His dad's up at the hospital with him. Jen's very upset. I don't suppose you could come over?"

I left the house immediately and walked briskly round

to Jen's. Cheryl opened the door and pointed to the kitchen so I went straight in.

"What happened?" I said.

Jen's face was red and there were several crunched-up tissues nearby. She told me the story in dribs and drabs.

Chris had spent the previous day with Karen, Jen said, leaving about ten to return home. Jen had just got back from Norfolk and was tired and hungry and managed to persuade Chris to go and pick up a pizza. An hour later he hadn't returned and Jen thought he had popped into the pub. When midnight came and he still wasn't back she and her dad went out walking in the direction of the takeaway. They didn't get very far. Passing an alleyway at the far end of the street they heard some moaning. They found Chris about twenty metres along, barely conscious, a lot of blood coming out of a cut near his eye. The ambulance came quickly and they took him to hospital. He needed stitches over his eye and he had some broken ribs and bruising.

I must have had a pained look on my face because Jen put her hand on my shoulder.

"I know," she said. "It's just awful. Poor Chris."

Cheryl came into the kitchen then and filled up the kettle. She was looking tired, her hair, usually perfectly styled, sticking up where it hadn't been combed.

"Who did it?" I asked.

"Chris was in too much of a state to say anything. My dad thinks it was probably a gang of lads drugged up or drunk. Or maybe someone was trying to steal his money. When I left the hospital there was a WPC waiting to talk to him. I knew her. She'd done a talk at college. About staying safe? You remember?" Jen looked at me. "Tall, blonde woman. WPC Clarke."

I nodded, vaguely remembering the woman she was referring to. The sound of the front door banging made us all sit up and look.

"That's my dad and Chris," Jen said.

But it wasn't. It was Jen's dad on his own. He walked into the kitchen with a stony face. Jen stood up and threw a load of questions at him. *Where's Chris? Is he still in hospital? Have they kept him in? Is he having an operation?* In the end her dad put his hand up to stop her.

"They're keeping him in until later this afternoon. He had a knock on the head and they're doing a scan to make sure there's no internal bleeding."

This made Jen worse.

"Internal bleeding!" she whispered, as though her dad had just confirmed it.

Her dad sat down heavily. He still had his coat on and he put the palm of his hand up to his forehead.

"Calm down, Jenny. They've put stitches around his eye and it doesn't look as though it's affected his sight in any way, so that's one good thing. He's still very shocked, though."

"Does he remember much about it?" I said.

"No. Not much. He was walking home with a pizza and he heard someone calling from down the alley. It sounded like they were in trouble, you know, ill or something, Chris said. When he got there there was no one. He turned to walk away and then he said someone jumped him from behind."

"But I thought he was mugged?" I said.

"That's what we all thought, but Chris says no. He says he was attacked from behind."

"How awful," Cheryl said.

"There was no demand for money, no threats. Chris says he didn't hear a word. He just felt an arm round his throat and some punches at his ribs."

"How many of them were there?" I said.

But he didn't answer. He was sitting quite still, his face passive except for a quiver at the edge of his lips. He was trying to stay calm, I could tell, his hand on the table closed tightly like a fist. He took a deep breath up through his nose.

"Came up on him from behind. You can't get much more cowardly than that!"

"How many did Chris say?" Cheryl said softly, reaching across and covering his ball of a fist with her hand.

"That's the funny thing. Chris says he thinks it was it was just one person. You'd think that that would make it a fair fight – if there's anything fair about this situation at all – one on one. But Chris isn't a fighting lad. He's tall but he's skinny. You know, he couldn't pack a punch."

"Just one person?" I said, a feeling of dread settling between my shoulders.

"Did he give the policewoman a description?" Jen said, her voice croaky.

"No. Chris didn't see the lad. He was behind him the whole time, and don't forget it was pitch dark."

Only one person. I sunk down in my chair. Paul Messenger's words came into my head, *I wanted to see the boyfriend*. He had followed me and waited outside Jen's so that he could see my boyfriend. *My best friend's brother*. I had told him this to get him out of my hair. *I have a boyfriend already*, I'd said, hoping that it would make him leave me alone, stop sending the letters, forget about me.

"Bastard!" Jen's dad said, through clenched teeth.

I couldn't wait to leave, although I promised I'd go back later in the day. I wanted to get home, back to my house, back to my room. I needed to be on my own so that I could think clearly. I kept my mind blank all along the streets, refusing to let my thoughts deal with what I had just heard. Opening my front door I heard the sounds of my mum and dad in the kitchen so I called out and went straight upstairs. Inside my room I stood very still, letting the tension drain out of me.

Paul Messenger beat up Chris Stoker. I knew it. He was there, in that alley, calling gently to Chris as he walked home with his pizza. He came up on him from behind and punched him in the ribs a few times before pushing him away so that he fell on to the hard ground and cut his eye.

The picture in my head made my legs go weak and I sat down on the very edge of the bed. This whole situation was much more serious than I had thought. It wasn't just me who was involved. Now someone else had been hurt.

The letter of resignation caught my eye. It was there up against the clock radio where I'd left it. I leaned over and picked it up. My resignation. This was the way that I was hoping to exit from this man's life. Trouble was, he wasn't planning on leaving mine. I closed my hand over it, crumpling the envelope. I lay back on the bed, a dragging feeling in my stomach. Paul Messenger was not going to go away by himself. I pulled my knees up towards my chest and buried my face in the duvet.

Something would have to be done.

Exactly an hour later, I was standing in the reception area of the police station and WPC Clarke was across the desk looking expectantly at me. She wasn't as tall as I remembered but then I had been sitting down when she gave her talk, *Staying Safe on the Streets*.

"You said you wanted to speak to me?" she said, briskly, her eye straying to a group of lads coming in the door.

"I can tell you who beat Chris Stoker up," I said.

SIXTEEN

I told WPC Clarke the whole story: the letters, Paul Messenger's attentions to me at the supermarket; seeing him outside work, at the gates of my college, across the road from Jen's house on that rainy night. I told her about my interview with him in the conference room, about finding him in the car park. *I can't help the way I feel about you*, he had said.

WPC Clarke sat opposite me across a table in the tiny room. The door was closed and there were no windows. It was quiet, not a sound, especially when she was making notes on a pad. At the side of the table was a tape recorder but we weren't using it. I wasn't making a formal statement. Not at that point. We were, in her words, *just having a chat*.

"He says he loves me," I said, shrugging my shoulders, managing a slight embarrassed laugh. "I've never given him any encouragement, not one bit. But he won't leave me alone."

She looked at me and nodded slowly. Her lips were turned up at the corners but she didn't look as though she was smiling. Her eyes were attentive but cold.

"So you told him Chris Stoker was your boyfriend?"

I nodded.

"Why did you do that?"

"At the time, when I first told Mr Messenger, I thought . . . I thought there might be a chance that he would be my boyfriend. That's the awful part," I said, giving another little laugh, "I thought, at first, I thought the letters were from Chris."

She didn't speak, just kept looking at me with that half-smile on her face.

"But they weren't."

"No."

I wasn't feeling comfortable at all. She was only the first person I had to tell. My mum and dad would be next, then Jen's family.

"You say there were six letters in all."

I nodded.

"And you don't have them any more?"

"No," I said, remembering the pile of ashes in the sink.

"OK, you can leave this with me," WPC Clarke said. "I'll discuss it with my colleague and then, I imagine, we will pay Paul Messenger a visit. Meanwhile. . ."

She paused for a moment, as if thinking hard.

"Meanwhile it would probably be better if you didn't see Mr Messenger, or contact him."

"I've got no intention of seeing him," I said, surprised at the request.

"We'll be in touch with you in a day or two, after we've looked into it." She flipped her notepad closed and stood up. I followed suit.

In a few minutes I was out on the street, the bright daylight making me screw up my eyes. I put my hand in my pocket and felt something there. I pulled out the crumpled white envelope, the words *Personnel Manager* across the front. There would be no need for me to present this letter any more, no need at all. Once the police had spoken to Paul Messenger it would be him who was out of work. I shoved it back into my pocket and walked off.

My mum and dad reacted differently. My dad was shocked and angry and kept standing up and walking to the window and back as though checking that Paul Messenger wasn't outside the house at that very moment. My mum just sat still, taking it all in, asking me things from time to time, saying, *Are you sure?* and looking puzzled as though I might have made some kind of mistake, as though I had misinterpreted the letters.

"Where are they?" she'd said. "Can I see them?"

When she heard that I'd got rid of them she raised her eyebrows with a hint of irritation. By that time, my dad had perched on the arm of the chair in which I was sitting, one of his arms loosely around my shoulder.

"He hasn't . . . tried to touch you . . . has he?" he said, amid several hollow coughs.

"No, no. Nothing like that. He just says he loves me. That's all."

My mum took a deep breath and then got up and went out of the room. A moment later she came back in with paper and a pen.

"Can you start at the beginning, love. I just want to get it all straight in my mind."

I told the story again. From behind I could hear my dad pacing up and down, opening and closing cupboard doors in the kitchen. When my mum was finished taking notes she called out and asked him to make a cup of tea. Then she put her paper and pen aside and spoke softly.

"You understand, don't you love, that there are these, I don't know what we'd call them, *damaged* people around. Maybe he is one of them. Maybe things have happened in his life that have made him very needy."

"But he's got a wife and baby," I said.

"That's right." She nodded. "He's to be pitied really, not feared."

"But he beat Chris up," I said.

"We don't know that for sure. We need to wait and see what the police say."

I didn't speak. Trust my mum to look at both sides. I wanted to argue back at her but I didn't have the energy. I was glad when my dad came in with the mugs of tea. She gave me a quick squeeze and then picked up her cup and went off upstairs. My dad seemed to wait for a minute until the door closed completely and her footsteps sounded on the stairs.

"I've got no pity for the bastard," he said, taking a gulp of tea and looking stonily down at the carpet.

Just after seven the three of us went round to Jen's house. My mum had made the arrangement earlier. Chris Stoker wasn't there. He'd come out of hospital earlier in the day and had wanted to go to his own mum's house. His dad had taken him there and was now back at home, looking a little less upset than I'd seen him earlier.

Cheryl showed us all into the living room and then my mum elbowed me lightly, as she'd planned to do before we came.

"I'll just go up and see what Jen's doing," I said, leaving them alone.

It was a relief not to have to tell them myself, I can't deny it. I was to spend time with Jen while they talked the whole thing through. The biggest relief of all was that Chris wasn't there to hear it. I found Jen sitting cross-legged on her bed and I explained what had happened.

"I remember that letter! You never said you got any more!"

"I didn't tell you because I thought they were from Chris. You're his sister."

"Poor Vicky," she said, taking it all in.

"The worst thing is I told him that Chris was my boyfriend and I think. . ."

"That he might be the one who beat Chris up?"

Jen was ahead of me, her face a picture of amazement. I nodded.

"And are the police going to arrest him?"

"I hope so," I said.

"What a creep!" Jen said, edging herself closer to me and putting her arm around my shoulder. "What a total creep."

On the way home the three of us were quiet for a while. I found myself walking slightly ahead, my hands in my pockets. My mum hadn't said much about how Jen's mum and dad had taken the news. I hadn't seen her dad but her mum had been really nice to me. She had brought up some tubs of ice cream which Jen had looked at and said, *Don't bother counting the calories!* Then she gave me a hug.

After a few streets I looked at my watch. It was just gone nine and I could hear my mum and dad talking quietly about work at their respective schools the next day. My dad was explaining about some new scheme he had to promote reading and my mum was trotting out some literacy targets that she'd read about since her promotion.

I was relieved that they had stopped talking about me and Paul Messenger. It made me feel a little less uneasy. As if the whole matter wasn't really that important and would soon fritter away without any further unpleasantness. It was true that Chris had been hurt, but Cheryl had said that there would be no lasting damage, just some bruising. The cut above his eye had only needed two stitches and would heal without causing a scar. The brain scan was normal and Chris had looked a lot better in the afternoon than he had the previous night. *Maybe,* Cheryl had said cheerfully, *Chris will be less careless about his own safety in future. Fancy walking into a dark alley in the dead of night!*

And Paul Messenger would certainly have to explain

himself to the police. Perhaps they were even in his house at that very moment. I tried to imagine the scene. They would probably want to speak to him on his own, so his wife and baby would be in another room. He would ask them to sit down and they would, WPC Clarke taking a seat first and then her colleague, whoever he or she was. At first, Paul Messenger would be pleasant and cheerful, but once he knew what they had come about he would be annoyed. He'd speak in loud whispers, afraid that his wife might hear. He'd be embarrassed, upset. Maybe he'd feel that I had betrayed him.

"Victoria."

My mum's voice broke into my thoughts.

"You were miles away."

"Yes," I said, dragging myself back to the present, to the dark streets and the three of us turning the corner at the top of our road, all quickening our steps to get home, out of the cold.

"College tomorrow?" my mum said, a little hesitantly.

"Yes," I said.

I so much wanted to get back to normal. There were two weeks before the Christmas break and I had assignments to finish. There were presents I had to buy and the end-of-term party to go to.

"You mustn't go back to that job," she said.

"I know. I've got no intention of going back there," I said, getting the front-door key ready, my mum and dad hanging back to let me in the garden gate first.

Just the thought of putting on my overall and heading for the till made me feel ill. Even if Paul Messenger got the sack or left voluntarily the place would have bad associations for me. I wondered if I'd even be able to shop there again.

I opened the front door and switched on the hall light. My mum took her coat off and hung it on the banister. She walked up the hall towards the kitchen.

"It's cold in here," I could hear her saying, "I'll just check the thermostat."

My dad was fiddling in his pockets, looking for something. I undid my coat, feeling oddly deflated. I'd got it off my chest and everything had turned out better than I thought it would, and yet I felt a little lost, directionless.

"The thermostat is fine," my mum was saying to herself and I heard her open the kitchen door and then felt a blast of cold air coming up the hall.

"What on earth?" I heard my mum's voice and walked down the hallway. "Oh, no!"

"What's wrong?" I said, pulling my coat around me.

"We've been burgled," she said.

The back door was hanging open and there was glass on the kitchen floor where someone had broken into the house.

SEVENTEEN

Nothing had been taken. That's why the police said they wouldn't come round until some time in the next couple of days. Although the back door was open and the window had been smashed it didn't look as though the burglar had had enough time to get any further.

My mum was upset, I could see, her face was drawn and she kept hooking her hair behind her ears.

"If it's not one thing it's another," she said, her voice low, apparently talking to herself.

She meant the trouble I had caused, I was sure. Even though the whole business with Paul Messenger had not been my fault I still felt responsible for the upset it had caused to everyone. So I found myself following her around while my dad was upstairs. I kept talking lightly, saying how good it was that we'd returned in time, trying to cheer her up. She didn't say much at first, she just made herself busy getting a torch and looking outside the back doors and into the near part of the garden. Then she came in and closed the back door tightly, turning the key even though there was a gaping hole, the cold night air spilling in.

I went with her as she walked through the downstairs, peering into the living room, looking closely at the television and DVD player. There was no sign that anything had been touched in the kitchen or any of the downstairs rooms. We went upstairs and found my dad in the study checking the computer stuff. It was all there, he said. The bedroom doors were all still closed and when we looked in them they were no different from the way we had left them. My mum and dad's was beautifully tidy; mine was a little messy, the duvet still rumpled from me lounging on it, my books and folders still dotted around the room.

The place was intact.

"We must have disturbed him as he was coming in," my mum said. "Lucky we didn't stay any longer at Jen's parents'."

My dad went out to the shed and returned with an offcut of wood. Squatting down, several nails wedged between his teeth, he fixed the piece over the area of broken glass. Then he swept up the mess and threw it in the outside bin. While my mum phoned the police he went to each of our neighbours and told them about the break-in.

Afterwards we all sat in the kitchen, my mum and dad with a large glass of wine each and me with a soft drink.

"Why do the police have to come?" I said. "If nothing's been taken."

"We need a report number for the insurance."

"Although we might not claim," my dad said. "A pane of glass. That's hardly worth the bother of filling in the forms!"

"It's important to inform the police, though," my mum

said, looking a lot calmer. "What if there were other burglaries in the area?"

We all went to bed at the same time. I didn't think I would sleep so I started to read a book. I couldn't concentrate, though, and in the end I put it face down on my bedside table and let the thoughts of the day float through my head. The whole business of Paul Messenger was finally out in the open. That was a relief. It was in someone else's hands. I thought about Chris and his bruised ribs, and then Jen came into my mind eating ice cream and telling me about all the things I had to look forward to over Christmas. I felt myself relaxing. After a while I must have dozed off.

The clock radio went off at seven thirty and I woke up and saw fingers of bright sunshine poking through the sides of my curtains. I could hear, from along the hallway, the sound of the shower and the footsteps of one or other of my parents walking downstairs. The smell of coffee was wafting through the house and I sat up, feeling refreshed. The dull, damp weekend was firmly in the past. I got out of bed and opened my curtains to let the sun fall through the window and on to the carpet.

I decided to make an effort with my dress and instead of wearing jeans I put some smart black trousers on and a newish top. I did my hair with the hot brush and put a bit of make-up on, smiling quickly at myself when I'd finished. I put my finger over the gap between my teeth to see what I'd look like if it wasn't there. Not that different.

When I got downstairs my mum was getting ready to leave for work and my dad was sitting behind the newspaper drinking some coffee. They seemed to be back to their old selves, my mum pulling folders together and making a face at the weight of her briefcase. She gave my dad a kiss and said, "Don't forget to ring the glazier," at which he nodded. Then she turned to me and said, "You should contact that policewoman today and see what's happened about that man." I nodded and she gave me a little wave and left. My dad went back to his newspaper and I got some cereal out and put it in a bowl. As I sat eating I looked at the back door. The wood covering the broken window was an eyesore but it would be fixed. Then we could forget that it had happened at all.

While my dad was upstairs getting his stuff together, I stood waiting in the hallway and had a look at myself in the full-length mirror by the door. The top and trousers were nice but the trainers ruined the whole look. My dad had disappeared into his study so I knew I had time to go and change into some black boots. I dashed upstairs and opened my wardrobe. The boots were on the bottom section of my shoe tidy and I had to kneel down and reach in to get them out. Sitting back, holding the boots, I felt a bit disorientated. Something looked odd, different. The bottom of my wardrobe looked strange, as if it were someone else's. I stood up and looked again. Something was definitely different, but I couldn't quite see what it was. Hearing my dad running down the stairs I sat on my bed, pulled my trainers off and put the boots on. Looking back to my wardrobe I realized what was wrong. My eyes scanned the hangers, and then each shelf, moving downwards until I got to the bottom. My red dress wasn't there. I had screwed it up after the party and put it at the bottom, nestled between a pair of shoes and a bag. It was gone. It simply wasn't there.

I heard my dad calling me from downstairs.

Had my mum found it and moved it somewhere?

"Coming!" I shouted and did a quick sweep of the room, looking under the bed, in the drawers, in the linen box.

It was nowhere. My red dress had vanished.

My dad's voice was getting a little tetchy.

"Vicky, I've got to go. I'm going to be late!"

But I wasn't going anywhere. I sat on my bed and kicked my discarded trainers out of the way. Someone had broken into our house. They hadn't stolen a thing, hadn't even got beyond the kitchen, we thought. It was just a random burglary, we thought.

But it wasn't. The man who had come in had only wanted something of mine. He had crept through the house without touching a thing. He'd gone upstairs and opened and closed each door until he'd found my room. What then? Had he just looked for the dress especially? Or had he considered other things, my books, my jewellery, my make-up? Had he sat at my desk? Or lain on my bed? In the end he had taken my red dress. He had seen me in it on the night of the party. He had singled it out for a mention in a letter.

Paul Messenger. In my house. In my room.

For the first time I felt truly scared.

EIGHTEEN

WPC Clarke arranged to come and see us at home a couple of days later. She wanted to talk to the three of us together, which, at the time, I didn't think was strange. I imagined that Paul Messenger would be brought in for questioning but my dad wasn't sure. I eventually got myself out to college. I turned up for a number of lessons but my heart wasn't in it. The rest of the time I sat with Jen in the canteen.

"I can't believe he broke into your house!" she said, for the tenth time. Then she settled herself into the chair and insisted that I go through the whole story again.

"Do you think he wants to hurt you?" Jen blurted out, her eyes glittering at the drama of it.

"No!" I said. "Why would he hurt me?"

"Because he can't have you?"

I shook my head. The thought hadn't entered my mind until that moment. I dismissed it immediately. I hadn't felt any physical fear of Paul Messenger. What I felt was something different entirely. I had this sense of him pushing his way into my life, like a lonely relative, or the child of some neighbour who is desperate to be friends. I felt sorry for him, embarrassed for him, slightly nauseated at his need. Most of all I just felt weighed down by him. Just like I'd felt when Jordan Hill had been hanging around. It was all too much. The letters that had once seemed like little rays of sunshine were now like dark clouds filling the sky.

"He did beat Chris up, after all."

"How is Chris?" I said, immediately feeling guilty for just thinking of myself.

"He's staying at his mum's. I guess he's OK. He sounded pretty cheerful on the phone."

"Are him and Karen. . .?"

Jen nodded solemnly before I finished speaking. I would have liked to ask her more but she started to talk about Sam and what they'd done in Norfolk the previous Saturday. I listened politely, although I had trouble concentrating.

When WPC Clarke came the next evening it was a relief. My mum showed her into the living room and offered tea. She wasn't in her uniform. She was still wearing her white shirt but she had a grey sweater and some dark trousers on. Over the top she had a grey puffa jacket which was hanging open. Her hair, which had looked neat and tidy at the station, had been blown about and looked fluffy and flyaway. She was carrying a shoulder bag and just looked like an office worker or a shop assistant.

"I think I should get straight to the point, Victoria. I visited Paul Messenger yesterday," she said, as soon as my mum brought the tea and sat down beside me. "And I have to tell you that he was very shocked, in fact, by what I had to say to him."

"*Shocked?* About what?" I said, a little surprised by her business-like voice and manner.

"About all of it. The letters, the attention, the break-in. Paul Messenger is mystified by your accusations."

"But. . ."

I heard my mum saying *Ssh*. . . and I looked round and noticed something odd. My mum looked very like a housewife that evening. She had no notepad in front of her, no pen with which to make points. My dad was looking uncomfortable as well, fiddling with the cushions and brushing crumbs off the arm of the sofa. He hadn't changed out of his suit either, he'd just taken his tie and jacket off.

Neither of them seemed surprised by WPC Clarke's comments. It hit me then. They'd both known what she was going to say. They'd already spoken to her and knew what her words were going to be.

"Paul Messenger denies that he ever sent you any letters."

"Oh."

"I'm going to be completely honest about it, Victoria. He says you've made the whole thing up."

I was quiet for a moment. I had expected all sorts of responses from Paul Messenger: acknowledgement, explanations, apologies, excuses. I hadn't expected him to deny it.

"But I spoke to him about it. In the conference room at work. He said he couldn't help the way he felt about me."

I said it with a smile on my face, only a hint of

indignation in my voice. At that point I was still feeling relaxed, assuming that WPC Clarke was on my side. I looked at my mum and dad and each of them gave me a little nervous smile.

"I'm afraid we only have your word for that, Victoria. Mr Messenger denies that he said any such thing. In fact. . ."

She stopped for a moment, as if she were weighing things up before speaking.

"Mr Messenger says that it was quite the opposite. He said that it was you who had a crush on him."

"But the letters," I said, dismally.

"That's the problem, Victoria. You don't have the letters."

I sat back, dismay on my face. I had burned most of the letters and thrown away the last one. I had wanted him out of my life and now I had no proof that he had ever tried to get into it.

"Did you show the letters to anyone?" my mum said.

"The first one. I showed the first one to Jen."

"Why didn't you show her others? That's what teenage girls do, isn't it?"

I looked at WPC Clarke. She was asking a question but she already knew the answer. Her words were softly spoken but the meaning was hard and clear. *You didn't show them to your friend because they didn't exist.*

"I thought they were from her brother. . ."

Inside I was feeling this horrible tightness, like something clinging to my ribs. I glanced at my mum and dad. My mum was frowning at me, but her mouth was soft and sympathetic, as though she was torn between two sets of feelings. My dad was looking down, his face expressionless.

They don't believe me either, I thought.

"You said that Mr Messenger waited for you on the street, outside Jennifer Stoker's house. Did you point him out to her?"

"No, she was upstairs. . ."

"And your father picked you up while Paul Messenger was standing there in the pouring rain."

I looked at Dad and he nodded.

"But you didn't say anything to him. You didn't say, *Dad, that man's been bothering me*."

"No," I said, my voice becoming quieter.

"And outside your college, you said he was standing at the gate waving at you."

I nodded, knowing what was coming.

"Did you point him out to anyone? Did you even tell anyone that he was there?"

I shook my head and sat quietly. There was a dryness in my throat and I felt this surge of self-righteousness. *How dare they*, I thought. I must have started to cry then because my mum moved closer and put her arm round me.

"I'm not making this up," I said.

That's when WPC Clarke seemed to change. She took her arms out of her puffa jacket and sighed deeply.

"I'm not saying you are making it up, Victoria. I'm

telling you what Paul Messenger says. It's our job to look at the facts, to ask questions, et cetera, et cetera. You told me that this man was always chatting to you at work, letting you go early? He says it's the other way round. That it's you who is always talking to him, asking him about his baby and his wife."

"Just to be polite. . ."

"He says that last Saturday, when he was in a training meeting, you asked a number of different people where he was. You even asked someone where he lived. Then when he was going home to his family you followed him out to the car park and tried to speak to him as he left."

"Is that true, love?" my dad spoke.

"Yes, but. . ."

"He's even offered to find the CCTV footage of the car park and show us."

I felt numb.

"What about Chris Stoker?" I heard my mum saying.

"Chris Stoker has no idea who beat him up. He doesn't remember a thing."

"And the break-in. Are you saying I've made that up?" I croaked.

"Not at all. You had a break-in, that's true. But there's no evidence to say it was Paul Messenger. In fact, his wife maintains that he was at home, with her, on both those occasions."

"My red dress is gone. It's the only thing that was taken."

"The thing is, Vicky. Me and your dad, we didn't even know that you had a red dress," my mum said.

I saw then how weak the whole thing looked. How pathetic.

"When we get a complaint like this we have to take it very seriously indeed. There's a man's life at stake here. His job, his wife, his child. We have to be absolutely sure."

"You don't believe me!"

"No, that's not true. I think you did receive some letters. I think that in looking for the sender you have perhaps allowed your imagination to get the better of you."

"I wasn't imagining it!"

"I phrased that badly. What I mean is that you were at work and this older man was kind to you. He showed you some attention and you put two and two together and thought the letters were from him."

"No," I said.

"But that's exactly what happened with your friend's brother. Isn't that what you told me? That you had assumed that the letters were from him. When they weren't you were upset. I can understand that."

"He told me to my face that he loved me! How could I make that up?"

"I think you've misunderstood him. Mr Messenger himself said you were upset by something and he tried to comfort you."

"Vicky, love, don't get upset."

My mum's voice sounded different: meek, apologetic.

"If we had some evidence it would be different. Meanwhile Mr Messenger has transferred to another store and I don't think you'll see or hear from him again. I would urge you to consider finding another job. Put all of this behind you. Make a fresh start."

I could hardly speak. I nodded a couple of times but that was just to finish the interview, to get rid of the woman.

"I want you to take my card. There's a direct-line number on there. If there's any problem then you can contact me immediately. In the meantime I'll continue with the investigation and if there's anything else you want to tell me about, feel free to ring."

They were nice words, but even as I took the card I knew I would never ring WPC Clarke. My mum showed her out and my dad got up and started to pace about. When she came back into the living room she looked nervous.

"Are you all right, love?" she said.

"You didn't believe me," I said, the tears slipping down my cheeks. "Neither of you."

They both looked defeated, as if I'd caught them out at something. For once my mum was quiet, no suggestions, no plans or strategies. I got up and left them to it.

NINETEEN

I was still reeling a couple of hours later. I was on my bed, my knees stiffly up in front of me, the duvet crumpled and untidy underneath. I was going over it all in my head. To me it was crystal clear. Paul Messenger had an unhealthy interest in me. Everyone else thought it was the other way around.

A couple of times I half rose off the bed to phone Jen but then I stopped. What was the point? What could I say to her? *They think I made it up.* Oh, she would be shocked and listen with her mouth open. She would disagree with the points they made and nod wholeheartedly whenever I insisted that my story was true. But in the end wouldn't she just see it as the others had? She had looked over the first letter, that was true, but might she not be in agreement with the policewoman? That I had misinterpreted it all?

I felt angry, and in the end I just sat festering about it all, tugging and pulling at my duvet, pushing myself back into the headboard of the bed.

About ten, I heard a timid knock on my bedroom door.

"Can I come in?" my mum said.

I didn't answer but the door opened anyway.

"I need to talk to you for a minute," she said, coming

across and sitting down on the edge of my bed. I didn't move at all.

"I don't know what's been happening here, Vick," she said. "But your dad and I have had several conversations with WPC Clarke and we've argued your side as much as possible. I don't want you to think that we didn't believe you."

I was silent, my feelings all tangled up inside.

"I just wish you'd come to me first, before going to the police station."

"What difference would that have made?" I said.

"We might have been able to do something. See the man privately, warn him off, I don't know. The minute the police arrived he must have seen the seriousness of it and had a story ready."

"You do believe me?" I said, surprised.

"Yes . . . no. I honestly don't know. It's not that I think you're lying. I know you wouldn't do that. I think you definitely believe this man has feelings for you. I know you did get some letters, I even think I remember one of them arriving. But do you think there's the tiniest possibility that you have misread the situation?"

I didn't answer. I forced myself to think back. *I can't help the way I feel about you*, he had said, as his car window closed. How could I have misread that? I shook my head, not trusting myself to speak. My mum sat very still for a minute and looked as though she was on brink of saying something a couple of times. Eventually she did speak.

"Do you remember when you were eleven and that lad from round the corner was bothering you?"

"Jordan?" I said.

"You said he was always hanging round and it was making you feel bad?"

I nodded, unsure about what was coming next.

"I went round to see his mum. To see if I could sort things out without hurting the lad's feelings?"

"You did," I said. "It was no problem after that."

"Trouble was," she said, "when I spoke to his mum she said that her son had been complaining that it was the opposite. That it wasn't him who was always hanging round. It was you."

I listened, letting the words sink in.

"You never said anything at the time."

"I didn't want to upset you," she said.

"It's not true, though. He was always there. Every time I turned the corner he was hanging around, waiting for me."

"That's what he said. His mum told me he was always complaining about it. Whenever he was with his friends at the bus stop or the sweet shop there you were. She told him to pull himself together."

"So you didn't believe me then, either!"

"I'm not saying that I didn't believe it. I just think people's perceptions are different. That's how it *seemed* to you. That's how it *seemed* to him."

"But he stopped hanging around as soon as you spoke to his mum!"

"Or you stopped looking for him. You stopped worrying about it so you didn't notice if he was around or not."

She was speaking gently, choosing her words with great care.

"I just want you to think about it for a few days. Could you possibly be overreacting to this man?"

I opened my mouth to speak but she put her hand up.

"Just think about it. Could the letters have come from somewhere else? You thought the sender was Christopher Stoker. When you found out it wasn't him you just latched on to the first kind adult nearby."

She stopped and I thought how easy it would be to please her. To just say, *Yes, you're right*. Then it would all go away.

"If after a couple of days you're still absolutely sure then Dad and I will go to the police ourselves and insist that something is done."

She got up then and I pushed myself further back into the headboard, pulling the duvet up around me even though I was still fully clothed.

When the door closed behind her I slumped down and turned the bedside light off. I wanted to lie in the dark, to wallow in the whole miserable situation. I thought I might even go to sleep like that, in my jeans, T-shirt and socks; just to make some kind of statement. Jordan Hill. Even a kid like that had thought that I was to blame. How had that happened? I tossed and turned and heard my mum and dad getting ready for bed next door. I didn't answer when each of them called out *Goodnight*. Why should I?

After what seemed like a long time I sat up. It was just after eleven but the house was quiet. There was just the occasional mumble from next door, the sound of my mum and dad chatting before they went off to sleep. I decided that I would have to get undressed after all. Maybe if I read for a while I could take my mind off it, possibly even go to sleep.

I peeled my jeans and socks off and then pulled my T-shirt over my head. I pulled a clean nightie out of the drawer and put it on. I immediately felt cooler, more relaxed. The streetlight was sending a glow through the window so I stood up and went across to close the curtains. I was feeling calmer altogether.

So what if he had denied it? I knew the truth. So what if he had persuaded the police that I was a liar? WPC Clarke said that he had transferred to another store. Didn't that in itself show that he was rattled? He knew I was telling the truth and wanted to avoid to seeing me. He was out of my life now, that was the main thing. So what if people thought that I was to blame? I could live with that as long as I didn't have to see him or speak to him again.

I pulled one curtain across and found myself staring out into the street. It was dark and quiet with just some lights on in the houses opposite. A few doors down a car pulled up and let out a young couple. The woman was walking to the front door of a house and the man was leaning in through the driver's window. It looked like he was paying his fare. He straightened up and tapped the roof with his hand and the car drove off. Then he followed the woman to the door where she was fiddling with her keys. He put his arms round her from behind and she seemed to crumple up with giggles. Then the door opened and they both tumbled in. I found myself smiling at their silliness and when the door closed I went to pull the other curtain across.

I saw him then. Standing across the road on the opposite pavement. It gave me a fright. He was there, partially hidden by a tree. All I could see was one side of his body and his face staring up at my window.

Paul Messenger. In my street. I felt sick.

I found myself walking backwards away from the window and I must have shouted out or screamed or something because in moments there was a lot of movement next door and then my mum and dad were in my room.

"He's out there. In the street. He's watching me," I said.

My dad, just wearing boxer shorts and a T-shirt, turned immediately away and I heard him running down the stairs. My mum, pulling her dressing gown around her shoulders, had her arm around me and was trying to pull me back towards the window so that she could see what was going on. I couldn't move, though. It seemed as though I was frozen to the spot.

The front door opened and I tensed. How long for?

I couldn't say. All I know is that some moments later I heard the door close again and the sound of my dad's footsteps coming slowly up the stairs, each one sounding heavier than the next. Finally the door opened and he came in.

"Did you see him?" I said.

He shook his head.

"There was no one out there, Vicky. No one. I looked up and down the street and there wasn't a soul."

"He must be hiding. In someone's front garden, behind a car. He must be there. I saw him."

From behind I heard the sound of the curtain being pulled and my mum's no-nonsense voice.

"Vicky, you come into our room to sleep tonight. Dad can sleep in here. We're all too tired now. We can talk about this in the morning."

"But I saw him," I said, my mum leading me out of my room by the hand, like a young child.

Neither of them answered.

TWENTY

I didn't go to college for the rest of that week. I said I was ill. It wasn't a lie. I had a headache and found it hard to eat. I slept a lot and even when I was awake I lay in bed flicking the remote and watching daytime television. My mum made noises about making an appointment at the doctor's and my dad kept chatting to me about my work, my plans for the future, my favourite type of music, food, holiday destination. Any subject would do, it seemed. Just so that we didn't have to talk about Paul Messenger or the police.

Jen came round on Thursday night and told me all the stuff that was going on in college. Ricky Fairfax was seen snogging a girl with red hair in the car park. Nobody was sure who it was, or even if it was a student at the college. Our tutor, Bob, had told them that he'd got a job in another college and wouldn't be back after Christmas. A couple of teachers had done a sponsored silence for a day to raise money for charity. There was to be a brilliant end-of-term Christmas disco.

The last thing I felt like going to was a party. I didn't say that to Jen because I couldn't get a word in edgeways. There was to be a proper disco with flashy lighting and a good sound system. Everyone was going. There would be a drinks and snack bar, but no alcohol. Jen said that didn't matter because everyone would sneak in something to drink.

"Is Sam coming?" I said, trying to break into her chatter about clothes and Christmas presents.

"Nope. It's just college students. No outsiders allowed."

"Does Sam mind?"

"He doesn't know. What's the point of telling him? I'll be seeing him a few days later. Did I tell you I'm going up to my aunt's for the week before Christmas?"

I shook my head and she carried on telling me all the details: where she was going to sleep, where she and Sam were going to go, whether or not she could persuade her mum and dad to allow Sam to come down for New Year as she hoped.

"Is Chris coming over at Christmas?"

She nodded. "Boxing Day."

There was a moment's quiet, as though my comment about Chris had thrown her off her conversational pathway. Then, as if suddenly remembering why I was off college, she started talking about Paul Messenger. I guessed, from the things she said, that word had got to her from my mum and dad about the police visit and the theory that I had made it all up.

"I believe you!" she said, stridently. "After all, I saw the first letter."

Her comment seemed to stir something inside me. I put my hand out and squeezed her arm. Trust Jen to stand by me on what now seemed the flimsiest of evidence.

"I thought of something," she went on. "About his wife."

"What?" I said, wearily.

"It's sick, really. I thought, maybe she doesn't know a thing about it. Maybe she thinks he's the perfect husband and he's this sicko who sends anonymous letters. . ." Jen shrugged her shoulders.

Later, after she had gone home and I was getting ready for bed, her words came back to me. Paul Messenger's wife. I hadn't really given the woman much thought. He had talked to me about her, in those early days, before I had known he was sending the letters. She had just had a baby, he'd said proudly and I suppose I had imagined some slightly built woman in her twenties. Brown hair, I had thought, and a pretty face. It had only been a momentary picture, I hadn't thought about it again. I was just being polite.

Then, in the conference room, he had said that it was a loveless marriage. That it was over, and they were only staying together until the finances were sorted out. Then I hadn't pictured her at all, I'd just seen this sort of shape, a woman cradling a baby, deserted by her husband.

What was she like, this Mrs Messenger? Had she any idea about her husband? Or was he as two-faced with her as he had been with the police?

"Goodnight, Vick." My mum's voice came from the hall landing.

"Night," I shouted, with fake heartiness.

Before turning the light off I walked across to the

window and pulled aside the curtain a few centimetres. I looked across the street to the spot where I'd seen him a couple of nights ago. It seemed darker than before, the sky heavy with clouds, no moon or stars to light up the street. The gardens opposite had high hedges. I'd noticed this over the last couple of nights, as I'd peered into the darkness looking for somewhere that he could have hidden. The street was also lined with parked cars, and he could have crouched down waiting for my dad to go away; a man in slippers, boxer shorts and a T-shirt wasn't going to go far on a cold December evening. Or he could have simply run away. The end of the street was only a couple of hundred metres. The minute he caught my eye he could have sprinted up the road, turned the corner before my dad even opened the front door.

I had seen him, I was sure of that. Now, though, the street was empty and I let the curtain drop back into place and went to bed.

Next morning I woke up early. My eyes sprang open at seven thirty, my usual time for waking up on a college day. I found myself getting up and dressed, feeling a current of energy buzzing through me. I got my stuff together and went out on to the landing. My mum saw me first.

"Vicky?" she said, looking surprised.

"Morning."

"Are you off to college?"

"Yep. I'm feeling a bit better today."

She smiled and continued into her study where I

heard her sorting through papers. I went downstairs and had some tea and toast. My dad came into the room, perking up as soon as he saw me dressed and eating. He didn't say anything, didn't ask if I was better or if I was all right. He just started humming.

As I left the house I felt brighter than I had for days. Something had happened to me overnight. Maybe it was the things that Jen had said, or maybe just the fact that she believed me. I had to speak up, stand up for myself. That's why I was going out. My mum and dad thought I was going to college. Let them.

I was going to Paul Messenger's house.

He lived at twenty Margaret Road. I got to the street just after nine, sure that he would have already left for work. I loitered along the pavement, going in and out of a sweetshop, buying some chewing gum, looking up and down, building my courage.

Eventually, I rang the bell of number twenty, my hand trembling with nerves. I could hear a dog barking from inside the house and then the door opened. A tall thin woman with very short dark hair stood there. She was drying her hands with a tea towel and looking curiously at me.

"Yes?" she said.

From behind I could hear some music and the smell of toast was in the air. The dog was still barking, scrabbling at some door to get out. In the hallway, just beside her, was a pushchair.

"Mrs Messenger?" I said.

"Yes?" she said, shoving the tea towel under one arm, her head turning slightly away to listen for something inside the house.

"I've come to see you about your husband," I said, a slight tremble in my voice.

"What?" she said, a frown flickering across her face. "Is everything all right? He's not been hurt?"

"No, no, nothing like that," I said. "It's just that I work with him and there's been a bit of trouble."

I felt awkward standing on her doorstep, trying to spit it out. She seemed to misunderstand me.

"He's at work at the moment."

"No, it's you I'd like to speak to. It'll only take a minute."

A look of annoyance crossed her face and she seemed to think for a moment.

"Well, I've not got much time. I'm due at the clinic in about forty minutes."

She held the front door open and I walked in. She headed for the kitchen and I followed. When the door opened the dog came running out, its tail wagging. I bent down and patted its head. In the kitchen, on the table, was a baby carrier. In it, fast asleep, was a small baby.

"What can I do for you?" she said, briskly.

She was standing back, away from me, any hint of friendliness gone. The dog padded over to her, wagging its tail. Then it turned and came back to me. I tried to ignore it and concentrate on Mrs Messenger. One second she looked as though she was steeling herself, the next, she looked completely calm.

"Mr Messenger is my supervisor and over the last couple of months he's been sending me letters."

She turned away from me for a moment and opened one of the wall cupboard doors. She took out a packet of cigarettes, flipped it open and took out a cigarette.

"He. . ." I hesitated. "He says he loves me."

The match sparked against the box and she fed it to the cigarette that was in her mouth. She inhaled and then turned away from the baby, blew smoke out into a far corner of the room.

"I believe he is unwell," I carried on, coughing slightly. "I don't believe he really knows what he's doing—"

I was about to go on and make excuses for him when she interrupted me.

"Have you got the letters with you?"

"No, I threw them away."

"And Paul signed them, did he?"

"No. No, they were anonymous but he told me that he sent them. And it's not just that. He's been hanging around. I've seen him outside my friend's house, outside my house. In fact, I think he beat up my friend's brother."

"Why?" she said, a look of incredulity on her face.

I felt shaky, my voice cracking as I spoke.

"He thought this lad was my boyfriend. I also think he broke into my house and took a dress of mine. A red party dress."

She was staring at me and I wavered, leaning down to

stroke the dog, glad to have something else to focus on for a minute.

"So, let me see," she said, with forced calm. "First he's sending anonymous letters. Then he's hanging round you in the street, then he beats your boyfriend up, now he's a burglar as well. What else has he done? Stolen the Crown jewels?"

I knew she was being sarcastic and I couldn't think of a thing to say. She seemed on the brink of telling me off but she took a deep breath and spoke:

"Look, love, he's told me about you. I'm sorry you have a thing for him but he's my husband and you really will have to leave."

She'd only smoked a fraction of the cigarette but she stubbed it out on the draining board. Her hands were shaking and she busied them by tidying up some cups and plates that were on the table.

"I've got the baby to sort out, see? If I don't get to clinic early there's a long queue. You go home. Find a boyfriend of your own age. That's the best thing."

The dog had retired to a basket by the side of the fridge. Mrs Messenger squatted down to stroke him and when she stood up she seemed to have pulled herself together. She opened the kitchen door for me and I walked out into the hall. She hooked the baby carrier over her arm and took a coat off a wall peg.

"I know you think I'm making this up, but I swear to you everything I've said is true," I said, my voice thick with frustration. "At least, I can't be absolutely sure that he beat my friend's brother up, but the rest of it, the letters, the fact that he was always around, the break-in at my house. Those things happened."

She zipped up an anorak and then lifted the baby up. I walked ahead and opened the front door. I wasn't crying but my eyes had glassed over. She saw that and it seemed to affect her because her voice softened.

"You girls," she said softly. "You mistake Paul's concern for love. He's just a nice man. He cares about people. You mustn't mistake those feelings for anything else."

Her front door closed and she took a moment to lock the Chubb. Then, edging me out of her gate, she walked off down the road, changing the baby carrier from arm to arm. In a few minutes she had turned the corner and was gone.

I stood still for a moment, letting her words replay in my head, *You girls*, she had said. *You mistake Paul's concern for love*. She had an unshakeable faith in her husband. She loved him. I wondered what his real feelings for her were.

As I walked away I held one thought in my head. *You girls*, she had said. *Girls*: plural. There had been someone else, some other girl before me. Perhaps someone who had received love letters just as I had done. I wasn't the only one.

It was an oddly comforting thought.

TWENTY-ONE

I found out about Heather Carter later that day.

After seeing Mrs Messenger I ended up at college. I went to all my lessons, fielding concerned enquiries about my health and the reason I'd been absent. At the end of the afternoon I decided, on the spur of the moment, to go into work, to give them my letter of resignation and pick up my things. Jen came as far as the high street with me.

"I'll come in with you," she said, when we were outside the store.

"There's no need. He's not there. I told you, he's transferred to another branch. I'll just pop this letter into Personnel, pick up the things from my locker and go home. You could come over to my house later."

She walked off with a wave and I went through the automatic doors into the bright lights of the supermarket. It was warm and cheerful with Christmassy music playing and the ceiling hanging with silver and gold fringes. A sign announced *See Father Christmas December 20th onwards!* None of it made me feel festive, and, even though I knew that Paul Messenger wasn't there, I still walked straight down the aisle with my eyes on the floor, willing myself to get in and out of the store as quickly as I could.

The letter of resignation was brief, explaining nothing. I put it into the *Personnel* tray in the office. It wouldn't make me look very good, just leaving on the spur of the moment, in the lead-up to Christmas, but I couldn't help that.

The staff area was empty apart from Mrs Lister who had her shoes off and her feet up on the seat opposite. She smiled at me and then went back to drinking from a mug. I began to clear my locker, taking out some magazines and an umbrella that been in there for months. I took out my overall and folded it up, laying it on a nearby chair. Then I noticed a carrier bag in the bottom. I pulled it out and remembered that it held the stuff that I had used on the night of Chris's party. I'd forgotten all about it. Inside was a damp towel, clothes, shoes and toiletries. I sighed with annoyance at having to carry it all home.

Mrs Lister came over.

"What's this? A spring clean?" she said, cheerfully, stretching her arms out as if she'd just had a nap.

"I'm leaving," I said.

"Oh, that's a shame! When?"

"Today. I've explained it in a letter."

"Goodness, that's a bit sudden!" she said.

"I know. I do have my reasons. But they're . . . you know. . ."

"We'll miss you. And I don't just mean on the checkouts! Can't you wait until after the holidays? Think of all the overtime you can earn. And there's the

Christmas party. You don't want to miss that!"

"No, really. I have to go."

I had my carrier bag in my hand and I closed the door of my locker over, leaving the key in it.

"Have you got another job?"

"Not at the moment."

"Why leave, then? Just like that? No one's upset you, have they? No one's been nasty to you?"

I shook my head. What was the point of saying anything?

"Ah well, good luck."

As she turned away and walked towards the door something occurred to me.

"Mrs Lister," I called out. "Can I ask you something?"

I picked up my rucksack and the carrier bag and walked after her.

"Sure, I'm on again in a minute or two. You could walk with me."

We zigzagged past trolleys and people stacking shelves. I nodded at a couple whom I knew and Mrs Lister smiled graciously at everyone she passed.

"Has anyone else left suddenly, say in the last year or so?" I said, trying to keep level with her.

"Left the job?" she said, looking thoughtful. "People are always leaving this place. Especially youngsters like yourself. We go to all the trouble of training them up and then they suddenly leave for something better or because their boyfriends want them to go to football on a Saturday afternoon."

"No, I mean, did anyone leave suddenly?"

She thought for a minute, her forehead crinkled up. A man with a pushchair manoeuvred around us and a woman with a basket over her arm knocked into me, saying several *sorries* before moving on.

"Only Heather Carter," Mrs Lister finally said. "That was a while ago."

Heather Carter. The name rang a bell. A face came into my head. A tall girl with short blonde hair and earrings like curtain rings. She'd been on one of the checkouts when I first went to work in the supermarket. I'd hadn't talked to her myself because we'd never been on a break at the same time. Then one week I noticed she wasn't there. I assumed she'd left. No one said anything and I never asked.

"She left in the middle of the day. Just came back from lunch and went. She didn't even empty her locker. I saw her in Charlie's? The café by the bus station? She didn't look all that happy there, either. Pay was probably worse as well!"

We were at the checkouts and I stood for a minute while she told the woman signing off the cash register that I was leaving.

"Never!" the woman said, and gave me a sympathetic look.

"Not even coming back for the Christmas party!" Mrs Lister added, as if this was further proof of insanity.

"I must go," I said, afraid that she was going to spread the word along the whole line of tills.

"Bye-bye, love."

"All the best, darling."

The two women waved as I walked out of the shop door. It was only five thirty but it was pitch dark and felt much colder than when I had gone into the shop. I went across the road and got into the crowd around the bus stop. I thought about Heather Carter leaving the supermarket abruptly, in the middle of the day, and ending up in a café clearing tables and doling out fry-ups. I wondered if she had also been driven away from her job by the assistant manager.

A bus turned the corner and I edged forward until it pulled up and I got on. I only had three stops so I perched on the end of a seat close to the automatic doors. There were three or four people standing, a couple of them with giant plastic bags full of Christmas presents. One man had a long slim box that said *Artificial Norwegian Singing Tree – twelve Christmas favourites to choose from.*

I hadn't done a thing about Christmas. I'd bought no presents or made any plans to go out. Nor had I nagged Mum and Dad about the decorations and tree as I usually did. I still had a couple of pieces of work to finish for college, which was unusual for me. My work was often given in days or weeks before the deadline. I remembered then the college party that Jen had talked about. It was only a few days away and I felt a stirring of interest. *Why not go?* I thought.

As I got off the bus I let my rucksack drop off my

shoulder and grabbed it by the handle. With my other hand I held the carrier, one bag balancing the other. They both seemed a lot heavier than when I had first left the supermarket. I walked away from the bus stop and then turned into a side road, leaving the sound of slow-moving traffic wheezing behind me. The street was dark, although every three or four houses there were coloured lights twinkling from the windows, some draped across trees and others in strips along the glass. Some were flashing on and off and one or two houses had Father Christmas shapes illuminating the walls. I couldn't help but smile. All the same I quickened my pace; my hands were feeling the cold and the plastic from the carrier bag was cutting into my skin. A couple of cars went slowly past, bobbing up and down over the speed humps, but apart from that the street was empty. Just before turning into my road I stopped to swap over bags.

It was when I was bending over that I heard the soft beat of running feet from somewhere behind. I picked my bags up again and continued to walk, veering to the inside of the pavement so that whoever it was could pass by.

The sound got louder and slower, each footfall heavier than the last, and finally I knew that the runner had stopped behind me. He wasn't so close, but I could hear his breath, deep and regular, drinking the air in. I had an awful feeling inside, as if my stomach was falling down some dark hole. I stopped walking, my back stiffening, my arms rigid, the two bags weighing them down like lead.

It was Paul Messenger. I was never more sure of anything, and the bile rose in my throat as I turned round to face him.

"What?" I said, stepping backwards.

Paul Messenger stood still, his face stony. He was wearing running clothes topped with a thermal hood that seemed to cover most of his head, just leaving a small oval for his face. He was hot, I could tell, but his breathing was steadying and he started to jiggle about on the spot as though he were loosening up.

I turned and walked on but I had only made a couple of steps before he caught me up, putting one arm around my shoulder and manhandling me towards a high garden wall.

"No," I said. "Stop!"

My voice rose but his hand suddenly went across my mouth and because my hands were full I wasn't able to struggle.

"Ssh. . ." he said. "Ssh. . ."

My back was against a wall and I was still stupidly holding both of my bags. He turned towards me, his chest flattening me back, his hand still lightly across my mouth. He was big and felt strong, as though he could crush me against the brickwork. Instead he just held me there, putting his head to the side of my face so that I could feel his hot breath burning my ear.

"Victoria," he whispered, "why did you have to tell everyone? It was our secret! Now it's all messed up!"

"I. . ."

I tried to speak but he just shushed me again. My hands finally opened and my bags dropped one by one on the pavement. He didn't flinch, didn't so much as flicker an eyelid.

I looked along the street in case anyone was coming. My eyes swivelled back and forth, taking in the dozens of tiny lights in people's windows, the edges of them blurring as I looked from one side to the other. In the distance I could see a couple of shapes, boys probably, walking along on the other side. I had no idea how long it would take them to level with us and even then we probably just looked like a couple having a kiss and cuddle.

"I love you," he said. "I told you that."

That was when I looked in his eyes, just pinpoints of darkness staring straight at me. He lifted his hand from my mouth and I felt the cold air on my skin. As I opened my mouth to speak he gave a tight shake of his head for me to keep quiet. At the corner of my vision I could see the shapes of the two young men and I thought if I could only hold him there, like that, until they came past, then I could shout out and they would see us.

But he kissed me then. Only for a second. His mouth just touching mine. I recoiled, pushing my head into the brick wall, clamping my lips together, tensing myself for what was to come. But he loosened his hold, and with his mouth close to my face he spoke in a harsh whisper:

"Don't ever come near my wife and baby again. If I hear that you've been near my house I'll hurt you, do you understand?"

I nodded, my head moving rapidly up and down, and he backed off and started running on the spot. In seconds he was gone, off up the street, and I was left slumped against the wall, my bags on the floor, using a trembling hand to wipe his kiss off my mouth. The young boys passed by laughing hard at something. They hadn't even noticed me.

TWENTY-TWO

Why me? I asked myself this question all weekend. I looked out of my bedroom window every so often, my eyes scanning the street, making sure he wasn't there. Why had he picked on me? There were a dozen or more girls of my age in the supermarket, several of them much more attractive than I was.

I was afraid. Before Friday I had felt oppressed by him. Now I was in fear of what he might do. I kept sitting in front of the mirror and looking at myself, using the back of my hand to wipe any trace of him from my mouth. I pulled my hair back off my face so that I looked stern. I put an old sloppy jumper on, and jogging trousers that were years old. I wanted to look different, maybe so that he would no longer notice me, or if he did he wouldn't like me any more. I considered having a haircut and buying some dark hair-dye to change my appearance, anything so that I didn't look like sweet Miss Victoria Halladay.

The only person I told was Jen and she spent a lot of the weekend around my house. When I explained the details she looked appalled. She asked questions and I had to tell her that no one had been in the street, no one had seen him pinning me up against a wall.

"So there are no witnesses?"

I shook my head dolefully and saw, for myself, the faintest suggestion of doubt on her face. It was there for a second or two, no more, just a momentary expression, and then she covered it up and talked around the subject again. I could have stopped her, put my hand on her arm, made her swear that she believed me – but what was the point? She would lie, she would stick up for me, but who could blame her for having doubts?

So we stayed in being pampered by my mum and dad who were still treating me with kid gloves after a difficult week. They were being kind and upbeat, offering takeaways and DVDs. The atmosphere was mildly suffocating.

That's why, on Sunday afternoon, I had to go out, and Jen insisted on coming with me. We went for a walk around the shopping centre and after gazing idly at pre-Christmas sales and window-shopping for gifts we found ourselves opposite the bus garage and Charlie's Café.

"Are you sure you want to do this?" Jen said doubtfully, looking in through the steamy window of the café.

I did. Up at the far end I could see a tall thin blonde girl clearing some tables. I went in and Jen followed me, peeling off to go to the counter and order a couple of teas. I walked straight up to the back, to where the blonde girl was stacking a tray with dirty cups, throwing the dregs into a tin bowl. When she saw me looking at her she stopped.

"I'm not serving at the moment. Sheila will. . ."

She pointed to the woman behind the counter.

"You're Heather, aren't you? You used to work in the same place as me?"

She looked puzzled and then I said the name of the supermarket.

"Yeah, I sort of remember you," she said, although I thought she was just being polite.

"You left some time ago. You just walked out one day. Mrs Lister told me."

"What's it to you?" she said, looking at her watch, her voice taking an unfriendly turn.

"I wanted to ask you," I said, "if you left because of Paul Messenger."

Her face hardened and she started to clear the cups more quickly.

"I'm really busy," she said.

"I just want to talk to you about him."

"Has he sent you? To say something to me?" she demanded, in a loud whisper.

"No, no, nothing like that. It's just that he's been sending me letters. . ."

My voice started to croak and she stopped what she was doing and looked closely at me. In her hand was a dirty white cup, hovering over the slops tin. After a moment she upended the cup and the tea splashed out.

"I'm on a break in about ten minutes," she said, "I'll meet you in the bus shelter."

Jen and I drank our tea quietly. For once Jen hadn't

bought any food and neither of us mentioned calories or diets. Jen seemed subdued, whether she was worried about me or just fed-up from spending a dreary weekend I didn't know. From time to time there was a faraway look in her eye and I thought she was probably thinking about Sam or some other boy that she had her sights on. We had been friends for years and in the last six months or so the presence of lads had driven us ever so slightly apart. Her great passion for Sam and her spontaneous desire for other convenient boys had made her a little preoccupied; my feelings for her brother and Paul Messenger's weird attachment to me held us at a distance. We still cared for each other, but there were barriers. I put my hand across the table and grabbed on to her arm.

"We're still best friends, aren't we?" I suddenly said, surprising myself.

She put her hand firmly over mine, her grasp strong and warm, "Course we are. We'll always be best friends."

I was grateful and near to tears. Just then I saw, out of the corner of my eye, Heather Carter taking her apron off and putting on a short leather jacket. One of her hands dived into a pocket and pulled out a pack of cigarettes. She said something to the woman behind the counter and then, without looking at me, walked out of the café. I got up to leave, Jen drank down the last of her tea and followed.

She was sitting on one of the seats by the 209 bus stop. There were several other people around but there was room on the seat. I sat beside her and Jen sat beside me.

"What do you want to know about *Mister* Messenger?" she said, inhaling from her cigarette.

"He's been bothering me, sending me letters, following me and stuff. I've been to the police but they don't believe me. He denies it. He's made me look like a liar."

Heather Carter pulled the cigarette out of her mouth and bunched up her lips. She was looking into the distance.

"Did he do the same with you?" I said, afraid that she wasn't going to answer.

"Nah," she said, nodding her head decisively. "He didn't send me any letters. It was much less romantic than that."

Jen perked up, giving me a look. I felt this jittery sensation in my chest and I was willing Heather to start talking. I sat up straight, eager to hear what she had to say.

"*Mister* Messenger was one of the people who interviewed me. When I started work he was really nice to me, chatting and asking me what shifts I wanted to go on and stuff. He'd be on the same break as me and he always seemed to finish at the same time as I did. Then one night he offered me a lift. It was pelting down with rain and honest to God I wish I'd never got into that car. . . ."

Jen slipped her arm through mine and I sat tensely waiting. A bus pulled up and the surrounding people shuffled on to it one by one. When the doors shut and it pulled itself away from the stop Heather Carter continued:

"He said he liked me a lot. He said his marriage was dead and that they were only living together until they sold their house. I was impressed by him. He was a supervisor, after all. I was flattered. I saw it as a big romance. I even let him kiss me."

She seemed to visibly shiver.

"He took me home regularly after that. Sometimes we parked round the corner from my house, sometimes we drove up the forest."

She paused as if remembering it. Her cigarette had almost burned down and she noticed it and threw it away carelessly. I watched it on the pavement, glowing for a minute and then fading away, the ashes dry and dead.

"One weekend I saw him with his wife. It was round here, actually, they were shopping, coming out of Marks & Spencer. He had his arm round her and they were laughing at something. And the funniest thing of all was that she was pregnant!"

I looked across the bus depot to the shopping centre beyond. I imagined Paul Messenger and his wife bursting through the swing doors of M&S, laughing at some joke, gripping carrier bags full of things for their baby.

"I pulled myself together. I was having problems at home anyway, my dad was very ill and my mum needed me around a lot. I told Paul Messenger that that was it and I didn't want any more lifts or anything. He was quite nice about it at first, but then he started phoning me up. He wouldn't leave me alone."

"Just like you, Vick," Jen said.

Heather Carter glanced at her watch, "I've got to go. I'm due back. . ."

"Is that all?" I said, mildly disappointed.

"All? It was enough! Honest to God, that man phoned me up every day, five, six, seven times. He phoned my mobile, sent me text-messages. He phoned me at home and when I told him to stop he said he couldn't help himself, that he loved me and had to be with me. Then I threatened the police and he stopped for a few days. But it all started again. So I organized different shifts at work, anything to avoid seeing him. I didn't know what else to do. My dad was having chemotherapy. I couldn't chance upsetting him or my mum. Not then. Anyway, he said he would stop but he didn't. Then he started phoning me and not speaking. All the time. Even at work, someone would say, *Phone, Heather,* and I'd answer it and no one would be there. He scared me. One day I just couldn't take it any more, so I walked out. Funnily enough, almost as soon as I left the job it all stopped. Out of sight, out of mind. Maybe that's what you should do!"

"I've already left," I said, in an excited voice. "But, the thing is, if you came down to the police station with me they could charge him with something. They don't believe me. But if you told them your story they couldn't deny it then!"

She shook her head decisively.

"Nah. I'm out of all that now. It's just history. Why rake over it again? I don't want my mum to know I was fooling around with a married bloke. It would upset her. Even now, all these months later. He's out of my life now. Now that you've left the supermarket he'll probably be out of yours as well."

"But doesn't that mean he'll just pick on someone else?" Jen said, softly.

"It's not my problem. I had him on my back for weeks. I was so glad to get away from him."

She stood up and walked away and Jen and I followed her. Just before she went into the café she stopped.

"I'm sorry for you but I can't do anything to help. I buried my dad a couple of months ago. My mum needs me and we don't need no trouble right now."

The café door closed and I felt myself lean against Jen. Heather Carter's dad had died. My own problems shrank to nothing beside that. How could I ask her to help me? I walked away from the café, feeling weighted down with misery. Jen walked quietly beside me and then linked her arm through mine.

"You can't let this bastard get you down," she said, her voice uncharacteristically hard and serious.

It was easy to say.

"You've got to get on top of it somehow. The more upset you get the more he has power over you. Heather

Carter is right. Most probably he will leave you alone now that you've left, but even if he doesn't you've got to go on with your life. If he knows you're sitting crying at home he knows he's won."

She made it sound like a contest. I wanted to argue back, to explain how unfairly matched we were, how he could win every time. She just didn't understand the awful feelings that were inside me, a sense of foreboding, that I was never going to get rid of this man, that he would always be there, over my shoulder, watching me from afar.

"Heather Carter got over him. I'll bet he's really galled about that."

I nodded. Heather had her own problems but she really didn't seem frightened or upset by Paul Messenger. If anything she seemed angry at him, ready for a row with him.

"But what if he just chooses someone else, some other girl to latch on to?"

Jen was quiet for a few moments as if this had floored her arguments. Could I, knowing what I knew, just walk away and let this man start all over again with someone else? We quickened our pace, heading away from the warmth and light of the shopping centre. It was just before four o'clock but it was already dark and had started to rain lightly, little pinpricks of cold. Over in the far corner of the sky I could see a lighter area, the darkness tinged with deep red.

"Maybe you should write a letter of complaint," Jen said.

I almost laughed.

"Who to? Customer Services?" I said.

"No, the personnel manager. Then they'd have it on file, you know, in case he ever tried it again."

I thought about it for a minute. A letter to personnel. The idea wasn't so silly. He had sent enough letters to me. Why not let them know what he was like? So what if he denied it and they believed him? There would always be that tiny bit of doubt in their minds.

"That's a really good idea," I said.

Jen was miles away, though, her chin bobbing to some tune in her head. She had already forgotten the whole thing. Most likely she was thinking about the Christmas party and who she would dance with, or who she would kiss under the mistletoe. I linked my arm through hers, feeling calmer than I had for ages.

TWENTY-THREE

I wanted to wear jeans and a jumper for the party but Jen wouldn't let me. She fished out a tight sparkly top that I had bought the previous Christmas. The neckline was quite low and it had thin straps that looked like chains. I felt funny putting it on, exposed, my arms and shoulders too bare. It was as if I'd gone back in time to the night of Chris's party, and I didn't want to be reminded of it. Jen wouldn't hear of me taking it off, though, and suggested a short skirt to go with it. I shook my head decisively and pulled on my jeans and high-heeled boots.

Jen was wearing a new pair of stretch trousers and a silky top. She'd had her hair trimmed at the hairdresser's and was wearing some earrings in the shape of tiny Christmas trees that flashed on and off from time to time. *Just for a joke*, she'd said, but knowing Jen I guessed it was a way of attracting attention.

We were eating chocolates from an early Christmas present of mine and drinking from our regular bottle of cold white fizzy wine. I had my CD player on loud and Jen was practising dancing with a glass in her hand, her earrings flashing on and off disconcertingly.

I'd posted the letter about Paul Messenger on my way to college a few days before. I'd sent it by registered post

166

so that it would have to be signed for. I felt good about it, as though in the act of writing I'd flushed it all out of my system and now it was somewhere else: on a desk, in a file, an item on a meeting agenda, a bit of whispered gossip around the shop.

My dad gave us a lift, making the usual joke about coming in with us and not being too old to enjoy a good disco. We both rolled our eyes and the mood was high, except for one awkward moment when we drove along the high road and passed the supermarket. I caught Jen looking at me and I tried a little smile and a shrug of the shoulders as if to say, *I'm fine, don't worry about me.* It affected me, though, a moment of tightness in my throat, then I swallowed hard and we seemed to speed away, leaving the shops behind us, and approached the area where the college was.

"I'll pick you up afterwards, if you like," my dad said, as I got out.

"No!" I said, rolling my eyes at Jen.

"Then promise me you and Jen will get a cab."

I nodded and took the ten-pound note that he was waving at me. Jen was already half a dozen strides away, straining to get closer to the party.

The disco was in the student common room. It seemed to take for ever to get there. We followed a number of other groups of students along the corridors of the college, our heels clicking along the wooden floors, the smell of make-up and perfume wafting along with us. We passed our regular teaching areas and then went on through unfamiliar territory, laboratories and equipment rooms, the science offices and quiet study areas. As we got nearer I could hear the music, just vague at first, then distinct, getting louder, making us quicken our steps in anticipation of the night ahead.

We took our coats off and put them on wire hangers on a clothes rail that someone had set up outside. I had my purse and comb inside a tiny black leather bag that hung loosely off my shoulder. Jen was holding a small bag, empty except for a bottle of gin that she had sneaked out from home. She went straight up to the drinks counter and bought two lemonades and we added some to each. The taste of the gin made me shiver, but it warmed my mouth and throat up quickly.

It was dark except for some flashing lights that came from the disco at the front. I saw a few familiar faces but mostly there were people I didn't know, students from other courses, people whom I had never spoken to. There were several members of staff, I noticed, mostly men. Our tutor, Bob, was there and I left Jen chatting to him while I wandered off to find some other kids from our year. The room was hotter than a sauna; the tightly packed dancers, the light show and the sound equipment making it steamy. For once I was glad that the doors were open on to the courtyard, letting cold air into the room. After having a couple of dances and polishing off a couple more gins I walked outside. I skirted round the smokers and went to the edge of the bushes where the cold air seemed at its freshest. I stood for a moment, breathing it in. The grass underfoot was crispy with the cold and the sky was a deep clear blue, the moon like a segment of pale fruit. A couple were half sitting, half lying on the bench, their faces joined in a long kiss. The lad was trying to unzip the girl's jacket and she was trying to stop him. Then he moved his hand down to her skirt but her hand shot down quickly to stop him there. The kiss didn't stop but the hand wrestling went on all the while. No one, it seemed, was paying any attention to them except me so I looked away, mildly embarrassed at having been so interested in the first place. My arms and shoulders began to feel cold, so I turned to make my way back into the party.

Across the courtyard, standing by one of the doors, I thought I saw someone who looked like Paul Messenger. I stopped with surprise and just then a couple of lads, drinking from cans of lager, bumped into me and with giggling apologies stumbled on to where they were heading. When I looked back the space by the door was empty. The nearest person was a large girl with white hair and black lipstick.

"There you are!"

I turned and saw Jen looking pleased with herself, holding two plastic cups of lemonade. She gave one to me and I took it in a distracted way and looked back over to the doors. There was no one there.

"What's up?" Jen said.

"Nothing."

I had made a mistake. It was dark and I'd had too

many quick drinks on top of the fizzy wine. The man was on my mind too much. I followed Jen towards the doors. Several of the partygoers had spilled out on to the courtyard and were dancing to the music. I passed Ricky Fairfax who was with a short dark girl. He gave me a smile, showing his perfect white teeth. After the way I'd treated him I was grateful for the attention. Inside, the room was heaving with people, the disco lights only visible through gyrating bodies and heads bobbing up and down.

"Look at Bob!" Jen shouted in my ear.

Our soon-to-be-ex tutor was slow-dancing with one of the older girls, a student I'd seen around but didn't know. They were sandwiched together, her arms tightly round him and his head flat on her hair.

"Rumour is, that's why he's leaving!" Jen said.

"What, he's *with* her?"

Jen nodded.

"Wow!" I said, surprised.

The music stopped unexpectedly, the flashing lights fading. A collective moan came from the dancers. Something had happened to the equipment or the power and for a few moments it was pitch dark. Then the ceiling lights snapped on and there was a gasp as the room lit up and people were blinking and covering their eyes as though they'd been in long hibernation. From up the front I could hear a number of commanding voices as people tried to fix the problem. Around me there were the sounds of conversations starting up, the voice of the person on the drinks counter and Jen calling across to someone she had just seen. I turned round to see who it was and my eyes swept past dozens of stranded party-goers waiting for the music to start again. They looked pale and dazed, the sparkle of their party dresses looking tacky under the bright lights, the lads' hair-gel too stiff by far. At that moment the flashing lights came on for a second and there was a blast of music and a cheer from the crowd.

I saw him then. Paul Messenger, standing against the far wall, looking through the dancers straight at me. I was startled and my fingers dug into the plastic cup I was holding. The room was suddenly dark again, the music surging back and the dancers swaying to the thumping beat.

Dismay washed over me. I hadn't been mistaken. The man was here at my college party. He was looking at me, watching me, spying on me. I stood on tiptoe to look for Jen but the room had become more tightly packed as people came in from outside to celebrate the return of the music and the lights. I let myself be pulled towards the drinks bar, intending to stay up that end of the room where there were some teachers around. I put my hand down to my bag and felt a fleeting touch as someone's fingers fluttered across my palm. I turned sharply round but there was only a crowd of young faces behind me. I stood very still for a moment, puffed up with indignation, my eyes darting here and there to see what I could see. That was when it got worse, a man's fingers, thick and rough, ran down my back, sliding from my skin on to the fabric of my top.

I spun round and faced him. Paul Messenger, wearing a denim jacket, looking like a teacher on a night off. I tried to take a step backwards but I couldn't move for the dancers. He smiled and leaned towards me, his mouth next to my ear.

"You look sexy," he said.

I didn't answer. I felt a low rumble of fear in my stomach. This man was never going to leave me alone. He was always going to be around. Part of me wanted to hit out at him. Instead I turned and forced my way through the crowd until I reached the main door. I stood with my shoulders rounded, my arms stiff with tension. I looked at the crowd of people closest to me and saw Jen talking to a couple of lads. Relief rippled through me. In a moment I was standing beside her.

"I've got to go," I said, breathlessly, my words drowned by the music.

"What?" she mouthed.

I put my mouth to her ear. "I've seen him. Paul Messenger! He's here. I've got to go."

She pulled me back towards the doors where it was quieter.

"It's only eleven. There's still an hour left!"

"I can't stay. He's here! It's ruined for me."

"Only if you let it. What if you just ignored him? What if you just acted like you didn't care?"

I looked at her with frustration. She didn't understand.

Either that or she simply didn't want to go. The lads she'd been talking to were looking in our direction.

"I can't. He's here, in this room. He makes me feel sick."

"But this is just running away. That means he's won. He's got control over you!"

"Look, you stay and I'll go!" I said.

I turned but felt her hand firmly on my arm.

"Oh, no. Wherever you go, I go," she said.

I was so grateful I could have cried. She stepped away for a moment and said something to the lads and then turned back to me. All the while my eyes were scanning the room to see if Paul Messenger was nearby. The flashing lights and darkness and the crowd made it almost impossible to see anything.

"We can finish the gin at home," Jen said pushing the doors open and sorting through the coats on the rail for hers. She pulled mine out and shoved it at me and then found her own. Draping it around her shoulders she walked off up the corridor and I followed her, immediately feeling a sense of guilt for dragging her away.

I linked my arm through hers and realized that she was a little unsteady on her feet. In the bright lights of the corridor I could see that her skin was flushed and her eyes looked a little distant. She'd obviously drunk more of the gin than I had. After a few moments she stopped suddenly as if she'd forgotten something.

"I'm just going to give that lad my phone number," she

said. "I'll be twenty seconds at the most. . ."

"No. . ." I said but she had slipped off back in the direction of the party.

I stood watching, a mixture of irritation and indecision making me stand still one minute and take a couple of steps back towards the party the next. How typical of her, I thought. How could she just put some lad whom she hardly knew before me, her best friend? I stood under the lights of the corridor feeling absolutely exposed, counting in my head the twenty seconds. After at least a minute I took a step to the side and leaned against the wall of one of the classrooms. A couple emerged from the party, a boy and a girl whom I didn't know. No sooner had the doors of the common room closed behind them than the lad had the girl up against the wall and was fervently kissing her.

For a moment I felt a pang of envy. How simple it would be if that were me, my arms hanging round the neck of a boy who had a passion for me. Someone who searched for me in the canteen, who waited for me after work, who talked about interesting things and made me laugh.

Why was that so difficult?

The sound of a door opening behind me cut into my thoughts. I glanced down at my watch. Jen had been gone for two or three minutes at least. I was on the brink of walking back to the party to drag her out when I heard a voice. It made my stomach drop.

"Victoria."

I turned round and there he was, standing in the doorway of one of the science rooms. Just a man in a denim jacket, but the sight of him made my knees go weak.

"I just want to talk to you," he said, stepping towards me, his arm reaching out for my hand.

I wasn't quick enough. I opened my mouth to shout out and tried to turn away at the same time but he was there, at my side, his arm around my shoulder, twisting me back towards the doorway.

"No," I said, my voice squeaking out, my arms limp.

But he was strong, his breath hot and heavy on the side of my head. In a couple of steps I was in the dark room with him.

TWENTY-FOUR

I couldn't scream or shout. Even though my mouth was hanging open I couldn't make any sounds. I couldn't even move for myself. Making sure the door was closed tightly, Paul Messenger positioned me with my back against it. I looked around, trying to avoid his face, trying not to respond to him in any way.

I was in a science preparation room. Along each side were glass-fronted cupboards and shelves holding Bunsen burners and glass beakers and other equipment. I looked back and forth as I felt his body close up against mine, his chest squashing me against the door. I stared past him, refusing to catch his eye, and all the while he was holding me by the shoulders as if he was afraid that I would slide down the door and crumple on to the floor. Opposite me were the outside windows. I made myself look out through them, my eyes searching for the road lights glowing in the distance.

"Victoria," he whispered, "if you only knew how long I've waited to be alone with you, like this."

He bent his head and began to kiss my face, small pecks on my forehead and cheek and then down on my neck. My arms were hanging limply and my hands were in tiny, useless fists. I closed my eyes and made myself think of the party. Jen would be out in a minute. She would see that I wasn't there and raise the alarm. I felt one of his hands let go of my shoulder, rubbing up and down my arm, causing my strap to fall down. His head rose up and he kissed me on the lips, just briefly, his mouth hot, his breath searing.

I was like a statue, up against the door, trying to block out what was happening. That was when I heard sounds from out in the corridor. Heels clacking against the floor, a voice calling my name.

"Vick? Vick? I'm coming!"

It was Jen. I turned my head and cleared my throat as though I was about to say something or shout.

"Ssh!"

Paul Messenger's hand went across my mouth. It was tight and hard, his fingers digging into my cheeks. The soft face, the kisses, the caressing fingers had disappeared, and he seemed like a tonne of bricks weighing me down.

"Vick!" Jen's voice got louder and I heard her swearing with annoyance.

We both stood very still for a few moments and then there was the sound of Jen's heels receding up the corridor. I listened hard, hoping that she was heading back to the party to tell someone, to borrow a mobile, to find our tutor, Bob. But after a few seconds I faced the awful realization that she was walking in the opposite direction, away from the party, out of the college. No doubt she thought that I had just gone on and she was following me. It would take her a while to reach the college entrance and see that I wasn't there. Five or ten minutes at least. A lifetime.

Paul Messenger had taken his hand away from my mouth and his body had eased off me.

"Don't be afraid, Victoria, I'm not going to hurt you. I wouldn't hurt you. I love you."

I pushed myself back into the wood of the door and made myself listen to the distant sounds of the party, the heavy beat of a song and then a smooth segue into the next number.

"I won't hurt you."

I could hear his voice in my ear and I could feel his hand moving down from my shoulder and pushing its way inside my top until it was on my breast. He seemed to shudder, his breath quickening. My knees felt weak and I must have slumped down because he hooked his hand under my arm so that I was still standing, and then he put his mouth on mine and pushed his hand down between my legs.

"Wait," I said, breaking my silence, coughing lightly, forcing myself to look at him.

His face was close to mine, his eyes looking hard and determined. I felt this rage deep down inside me, a tiny spark that was burning my chest. What right did he have to do this to me?

"Wait," I said, standing up, pulling myself together. "I'm not comfortable standing here. Maybe we should. . ." I pointed to the floor and he looked at me with barely disguised delight.

He stepped back, away from me, and I was able to draw myself up. For a moment I felt tall and strong and using every bit of strength I had I put my two hands up in front of me and shoved him hard. He hadn't expected it and he fell backwards, flat on to the floor.

I didn't wait.

I turned and opened the door and went out. In one direction was the long empty corridor and Jen. In the other was the party. I made a decision and ran towards the music, past the rack with the coats, and dived into the partygoers, wading through the dancers, looking to the right and left to see if Bob was there. It was too dark, though, and I was propelled by a sense of panic to the back doors. Stepping outside I glanced back. I had no idea if Paul Messenger was following me, I could see nothing in the mass of dancers so I turned and kept going, through the smokers, past the kissing couples, past some people who were secreted in the bushes, until I got to the perimeter wall. I stood for a moment, catching my breath, not knowing what to do, where to go.

Perhaps he had knocked himself out and was still lying on the floor of the tiny science room. Or possibly he had cut his losses and gone home.

But after a moment, I saw, among the partygoers, a figure, moving quickly and with purpose in my direction. It had to be him. I knew that. In a second I was over the perimeter wall and on the pavement. I didn't stop but ran out into the road, one of my boots snagging on the kerb, the heel breaking loose and forcing me to limp across and hold on to one of the bollards. Cars whizzed by, going in both directions. I looked back and saw him hesitating at the wall. I caught his eye and I felt a surge of pure hatred for the man. He raised his leg to get over the wall and I panicked and backed off the bollards, one foot stepping behind the other, oblivious of the traffic.

I didn't notice the motorbike come round the bend, its driver low to the ground like someone racing at a speedway. It had its headlight on but I didn't see it, most probably because I was crying and the lights everywhere were looking blurred. It was making a roaring sound but I didn't hear it. All I could hear was the sound of Paul Messenger's voice in my ear: *I won't hurt you. I love you.* When the bang came I didn't feel anything. I was still feeling his fingers on my skin and his breath scorching my neck.

Paul Messenger felt it, though. I watched as the motorbike hit him full on and knocked him into the air. The bike veered off in a skid, its brakes screaming until it came to a stop further up the road. Paul Messenger hit the ground with a thick thudding sound. I looked away for just an instant.

I was numb. I had no feelings about it. I just stood at the edge of the road, looking across at his crumpled-up body, hearing the footsteps of the motorbike rider running back to see what had happened.

I didn't care whether he was dead or alive.

TWENTY-FIVE

Paul Messenger was kept in hospital for five days. He had a broken femur, knee injuries and a fractured skull. He was lucky to be alive, my mum said. I didn't say anything. On the day he was sent home from hospital WPC Clarke visited us for the third time. Her attitude had changed and she was awash with apologies. *Call me Miriam*, she kept saying, every time one of us addressed her. My mum opened the front door and I could hear snatches of a conversation about how tough it was being on duty over the Christmas period. *I'm not officially on duty*, I could hear WPC Clarke replying.

I was sitting in the living room, in the chair next to the television. I was dressed, for a change. I'd spent most of Christmas in my nightclothes. I wasn't ill; I hadn't been hurt and I didn't need to see a doctor. I didn't go out anywhere, though, and I felt most comfortable in my warm clingy pyjamas and my giant towelling dressing gown with the hood up.

That was my Christmas.

"Hello, Victoria. How are you today?" WPC Clarke said.

She hadn't worn her uniform for any of her visits and that day was no exception. She had trousers with boots and a giant pink fleece top which looked like a

Christmas present. She was carrying a small holdall.

"I'm fine," I said.

I was OK, if a little shaken. *Shaken not stirred*, my dad kept saying, trying to make me laugh.

"I just popped in to keep you abreast of developments," she said.

"Have you arrested him?" my mum said, firmly.

"We're looking into it. There are several possibilities, and as soon as the detective in charge makes a final decision you'll be the first to know."

We were top of their list, the first to be told, the most important people in the case. How different it had been only a week or so before, when nobody believed me.

"What will the charges be?"

I heard my dad's voice and then the door opened, and he appeared carrying a tray of mugs.

"That's the problem. We could possibly charge him for assault, he did, after all, try to kiss you and touch you against your will. On the other hand it will be his word against yours. He's already said that he misunderstood, he made a mistake. He thought you wanted his advances, et cetera, et cetera. . ."

I nodded, a feeling of distaste settling on me.

"He did harass you, we know that now, and we could charge him with it, but I think the courts would just throw it out. Sending letters is not a crime. Being around your street and outside your college is not a crime. He will probably say that he thought you wanted him there."

"What about the assault on Christopher Stoker?"

"He denies it. And there's no evidence to say it was him."

"So he can make Vicky's life a misery and not be charged with anything."

"We don't know. My superior is looking into what charges he can bring."

WPC Clarke shrugged. My dad swore, and my mum looked as though she was going to tell him off but then changed her mind.

"The burglary?" she said, with a hopeless look.

"Now that's where there is good news," the policewoman said. "Mrs Messenger? She came up to the police station this morning and threw this down on the counter."

There was a lot of crinkling as she pulled a see-through plastic bag out of her holdall. She laid it on the coffee table. It held a wrinkled and grubby garment, small and floaty. My red dress.

"This is yours?" my mum said, with surprise.

I nodded.

"That man's wife gave it to you?" my dad said.

"She found it in the boot of her husband's car, bundled up, stuffed in the middle of the spare tyre. It's pretty good proof that he carried out the break-in."

"So you can charge him with that?" my mum said with some conviction in her voice.

"We *can*," WPC Clarke said, cagily, "but even if it goes to court – and I don't know that it will – he'll just get a fine or some community service. It's a first offence, you see."

I found my voice after what seemed like a long period of quiet.

"So he'll get away with it?"

"Not entirely. Although he may, if we simply try and pursue it from the criminal angle."

"I don't understand," my dad said.

"If Victoria makes a comprehensive statement and swears an affidavit, we could try and get a court order to prevent him coming anywhere near her. Say, for example, that he may not come within a mile of her home or her college. It's called an injunction."

"That's hardly punishment," my dad said.

"But it means he cannot come near her and if he does he will go to prison."

"What about if he approaches some other girl?"

"That's something we're not in a position to do anything about. But his life will change dramatically after this. He'll probably lose his job, and hence his position of responsibility. And if he gets another he'll be under constant watch. The fact is, Victoria, this man needs some help, and we'll be arguing that along with the court order he should seek medical treatment and counselling."

"And that's the best you can do?"

"In the circumstances, yes. His wife's left him over all this. He won't just shrug it off and find the next girl."

I thought of Heather Carter then. I hadn't told anyone about her situation and I didn't intend to. I kept remembering her dead dad. The last thing she needed was to be dragged into this.

"So, it's over," I said.

"I'd be very surprised if you ever saw him again."

A moment's quiet settled on the room. In the corner the Christmas tree twinkled innocently. Then the policewoman got up to go, taking the plastic bag with the red dress and putting it back into her holdall. She gave me a smile and a little wave before walking out of the room.

"Thanks for coming round, Constable Clarke," my mum said, following her out, her voice a little stiff.

Please, do call me Miriam, I heard and then the front door clicked shut.

In the new year I returned to college and got on with my course and my studies. After my near accident at the Christmas party everyone seemed to know me and I was constantly chatting to new people, girls and lads, who seemed to find me interesting. Jen was always there at my side; whether to protect me or to bask in my glory, I couldn't say for sure. I was glad of it anyway.

I never saw Paul Messenger again. I heard that he'd got back together with his wife and moved to Birmingham. Miriam Clarke said that he'd come through his treatment well and had regretted what he'd done. The policewoman had been pleased with the way things had turned out, she told me. Just to be on the safe side, though, she'd telephoned an officer she knew in the Midlands and told her about him, just for their records, she'd said.

In the canteen, Jen and I talked about it from time to time. More often than not, though, Jen was on some sort of diet and we were more concerned with counting calories.

When I was on my own, at night, standing by my bedroom window, I thought of him. Looking out at the street below, I often saw the shape of him by a lamp post, his shadow by a car, a flash of movement as he jogged past. He was hundreds of miles away, I knew, but in my head he would always be around, watching me. It was something I learned to live with.

DON'T MISS

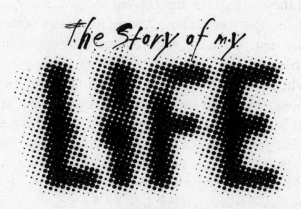

The Story of my **LIFE**

by Anne Cassidy

Kenny Harris is about to begin the longest night of his life. The stakes are huge, not just for him, his family and his girlfriend, but also for the man whose fate lies in his hands. . .

It all starts when he bumps into Nat on the tube platform one chilly September Saturday. Nat. His brother's girlfriend. Gorgeous and definitely not available. But something is set in motion that day, something that leads Kenny back to the same tube station three months later and the start of that terrible night.

Because it's also the day that he meets Mack. And his life takes a violent swerve in a completely unexpected direction. A simple, chance meeting that could destroy his whole world. . .